Domestic
Apparition

by Meg Tuite

San Francisco Bay Press 2011

Domestic Apparition
copyright (c) 2011 by Meg Tuite
All Rights Reserved

Manufactured in the United States of America
Editor: Robert P. Arthur
Designer: Jeff Hewitt

SFBP Paperback Edition
Library of Congress Cataloguing in Publication Data
Tuite, Meg ; "Domestic Apparition"

ISBN: 978-0-9828295-2-3

♡ Dearest Pat,

Love, Love, Love ya!

So happy to have you
as a great friend
and inspiration as
a writer ♡

Love, Lov ya,

Meg xoxo

Table of Contents

Acknowledgements

I would like to thank all the editors who first published these chapters as stories and flash fiction, including Jeff Hewitt, Ken Robidoux, Miriam Sagan, Jane Callahan, Nancy Stohlman and Kona Morris, Martin Chipperfield and Trace Sheridan Swan, Ryan W. Bradley, Sandy Raschke, Stephanie Bryant Anderson and April Michelle Bratten, Jennifer Parsons, Josh Goller, Tyler Bigney and Brittany Fenerty, Susan Solomon, Steven Seighman, David Fraser and David Elswick.

The stories have appeared in the following literary magazine and journals and I am grateful to all of them for their support: Lady Jane's Miscellany, The Santa Fe Literary Review, Hawaii Review, Connotation Press, Fast Forward Press, 34th Parallel Magazine, Calliope, Boston Literary Magazine, Sleet Magazine, Monkeybicycle, Sententia Magazine, Nova Scotia Review, Molotov Cocktail, Up the Staircase Quarterly and Luna Station Quarterly. "Family Conference" was a finalist in the Glimmer Train's Aug. 2010 Short Story Contest for New Writers.

I also want to express my indebted gratitude to all the outstanding writing instructors I've been fortunate enough to have worked with: Melissa Pritchard, Dorothy Allison, Miriam Sagan and Julia Goldberg to name a few and my heartfelt thanks to Karen Stefano, Kona Morris, Ken Murray, Pat Barnes, Heidi Schulman, Ken McPherson and all the unnamed readers and editors who took the time to read and send me editorial comments.

My utmost appreciation and lifelong servitude to Robert Arthur and Jeff Hewitt for editing and publishing this novel.

Thank you to my friends and family for all your support throughout the years of writing, especially my Dad, my brothers Kevin, Matt and Jeremy and my sisters, Bev, Annie and Josie.

This book is dedicated to my husband, Paolo, without whom it would never have come into existence, and my mother, Violet, who taught me the deep love for reading and writing.

Domestic
Apparition

SINISTER AGE OF THE DRAFT

When I turned six I became victim to one of the many human abuses of dumping a child out of the back of a station wagon into the snot-filled clutches of a pack of anonymous kids. It was an enforced group dynamics that came with all its paranoids, masochists and victims for no other reason then that we had turned the same sinister age of the draft, and as it was a Catholic school in the early sixties, abuse was not only condoned, but expected at any and all levels.

The teacher was a myopic, old woman with a pink barrette and brown teeth who spent a large portion of her day trying to figure out what her pension would be if she quit that afternoon, punching numbers into an adding machine, picking it up and sneering at it as reality spread bitterness over her face, while we were left to ourselves -a sort of Lord of the Flies meets Mickey Mouse -in which the forces of evil press in on the good like white bread on peanut butter. The so-called good, a weak but whiny lot who actually clung to that abstract of "justice for all," would tattle to Mrs. Pufry. "...Mzz Puffy, she hit me...Mzz Puffy he said the bad word...Mzz Puffy, I gotta go...Mzz Puffy, Thomas is hanging in the cloakroom again..." and Mrs. Pufry's hand would absently lash out at the sniveling chorus and shoo them back to their seats without looking up, including the one who had to go, who was now shamed into retreat with the rest of them, finding out early in life that time was never to be on his side as he fought a losing battle with the vicious stream that laughed its way down his pant legs.

After lunch and regulated nap, Mrs. Pufry would suddenly lurch up out of her chair and stumble toward the supply cabinets, like some hideous, reanimated corpse, and hurl herself around the room throwing out instructions, crayons, construction paper, and panic, forcing an art deadline on all of us. The class experienced its first creative block, staring at the paper, a pile of broken crayons, the clock that rushed around in a circle none of us could decipher, and Mrs. Pufry, now looming over us, pacing the aisles, staring down at the feeble slashes and stick men with disgust, cuffing a few heads yelling, "hurry up, fill that page, nobody asked for Picasso."

When the final bell finally rang at three o'clock and our parents lined up outside for their wards, each shaky child clutched a lopsided monkey, tortured landscapes, family portraits with a member or two missing, heads without bodies, bodies without heads, in what could have been a fair rendition of the birth, or at the very least, the first mass movement toward minimalism. School turned out to be a daily workshop in human dynamics.

A THOUSAND FACES OF A WARRIOR

When I actually got my own room I always kept the door closed. It wasn't like there was anything actually happening in there -I was usually reading -but the thought that something could or might be happening at any moment in my room made it a necessity to keep the door closed and everyone else out and wondering.

One afternoon I was lying on my bed reading a book that promised to launch me out of this reality into a place far, far away, when there was a knock at the door. It wasn't exactly a knock so much as a cautious, little tap. In other words, it was my mother. I let her stand out there for a while before I opened the door. I was fifteen, after all, and if something was happening in my room I had to give myself time to hide whatever it was I wasn't doing, and give her time to conjure up the worst of worst fears about what I could have been doing. I slammed drawers, closed my closet and opened the window before opening the door.

"What," I said.

My mother stood before me with a shoebox in her hands. She appeared more frightened than usual. Her eyes blinked rapidly like she'd just been hit. Her mouth was barely a mouth, wafer-sliced and shriveled. Her tongue flickered over chapped lips.

"Help me," she said.

"What," I said.

"Help me," she said. Her hands were shaking. "It's your sister," she said. She handed me the box. I took it in my two hands, held it in front of me and stared at it.

"I give up," she said. She turned and went back down the stairs. I watched her go. Then I closed my door, sat down on the floor with my back against the bed, and opened the box.

My sister was eighteen. I had two other sisters, but I knew which one my mother was talking about. Stephanie. No one in the family stirred up more frenzy. Sometimes she let me hang around and study her up close. One day after school she came home with a nickel bag of pot. She took me by the hand up to the attic, and said, "Let's smoke it all. NOW." I did whatever she said. We sat across from each other on a window seat that looked out over the backyard and the alley beyond, and rolled joint after joint. Then we lit them up, one after another, and smoked and smoked and smoked every last one of them. I remember our mom coming up to the attic at some point and yelling at us. I don't know how many hours we were up there. My cheeks hurt from laughing my ass off. It's all I could do. Stephanie talked. She ignored our mother and eventually mom went away, as usual, while Stephanie kept right on telling stories. My sister didn't talk like anyone else. She was either a genius or a lunatic, like my brother Nathan, I couldn't tell, but she had her own special language like no one I'd ever heard before. She'd say things like, "that girl was the tallest building I ever lived in," or after a date with some guy, she'd say, "I invaded the miserable casualty until he was a cornucopia of brazen limbs." I remember that line because I had to look up the words cornucopia and brazen after she was gone. I never quite knew what she meant, but I was sure it was something brilliant. After she totaled our dad's mid-life crisis Spiderman sport's car she actually quoted from one of her favorite, obscure writers while dad beat the shit out of her. She stared him straight in his veined, purpled face and yelled, "Looking down the barrel of your eye, I see the body of a Bloody Cinderella come whirling up!"

I loved Stephanie. She was translucent and mad. She could say or do anything and no one broke her down. Not even dad, and I was scared shitless of him. She stood up to him like some kind of hardcore warrior and I swear I could almost see a black cape flung across her back with her hands on her hips whenever she came into a room, daring him to trample her.

I could be stepped on. I was sickly thin and pregnant with terror. Dad would lift his hand anywhere within my vicinity and I would crouch in horror and go spasmodic. I had a few friends at school who were just as brutal. They would dare me to do stupid things like throw rocks through a revolving door into a store or tell this bad-ass teacher, who had greasy, blonde hair, that the wet-head was dead. I did anything they asked me to do just to be a part of their group. Desperation couldn't be hidden. I followed them around like a dog begging for a kick.

Stephanie was of a different breed. She was the innovator. Everyone filed in behind her like she was some kind of pied piper and I got in that line whenever I could. She still kicked me in the ass just like everybody else. When she was dangerous, she was ruthless. She beat me over the head with one of those miniature baseball bats they hand out at baseball games just because I wore a pair of her shoes one day. I wasn't a complete wimp, though. I'd bide my time and plan a counterattack whenever things had gone too far and it was needed. I would allow a certain period of time to pass after she'd nailed me for something. When she was way past the stage of suspicion, which could sometimes last up to a couple of weeks, I'd set my trap. I'd wait until the parents were out and Stephanie was lying on the couch, all comfortable with her feet up, reading a book or passing out. I'd stock the bathroom with peanut butter sandwiches, Kool-Aid, and some books. I'd make sure I was well supplied and able to survive until one of our parents returned, preferably dad. She had these long, precious brown pigtails she cherished that I wanted to chop off, but I knew dad would kill me if I did, so I knew I had to damage her, without permanent damage to myself. I would sneak up on her from behind when she was finally falling asleep and punch her in the face and yank one of those damn, stupid pigtails as hard as I could and run like hell. She'd jump up screeching and flailing to get at me. I'd race up those stairs three at a time with her close on my ass, screaming for blood, but I always got in there and locked that door before her body slammed against it. She'd pound for a while, and wail and tell me how she was going to kill me when I got out, because I couldn't stay in there forever. My heart would pump with her threats, just thinking of facing her again. When dad got home he'd tell her to shut-up and leave me alone. That was the good thing about not being Stephanie. She always took the crap from our parents whenever she tried to tattle on any of us.

But I always got it back. At night she'd sneak into my room and smother me with a pillow or pound me with her fist or ravage me with an Indian rub till I was sobbing. I never got the last word, but knew I had to try.

I stared at the open shoebox and remembered the only other time I had seen my mother with that same ghoulish look on her face. It was about six months earlier. I heard screaming and yelling coming from the kitchen. It was Stephanie and mom badgering each other, which wasn't unusual, so I didn't focus in right away. Then I heard strange words coming out of Stephanie, also not unusual, except these specific words held me captive.

"You're damn right I'm a lesbian, Lucy, and proud of it, you yodeling, apron-fested prig! So what's it going to be? You finally throwing me out?" Stephanie was threatening mom and loved calling her by her first name.

"I'm going to tell your sisters! How would you like that?" mom asked in a shaky voice. "I'm going to go in there and gather them round and tell them just who and what you are. We'll see what they think of you then," mom managed to spit out.

I was the only sister awake at the time. The other two were younger, and already passed out. It was a Saturday night and Stephanie was drunk, but looked scared when mom called me into the kitchen. I was scared too. I thought I knew what a lesbian was, but wasn't sure.

"Look at your sister, the one you're so proud of! Your sister Stephanie, the freak! She has sex with Alexandra on those little overnighters they do together. She's what they call a lesbian -obviously not like the rest of us. What do you think of that?" mom demanded of me. She was all twitchy and red. She studied my face to see which way I'd go.

"But then, look at you! Maybe you'll be one of them too, following your sister around the way you do. Maybe you're just another freak like her," mom screeched with tears in her eyes.

I had never seen mom like this before. She would yell at us when we got home late or stole her cigarettes or money, but I'd never seen her so outraged. She scared the hell out of me. This was another part of her that didn't show it's ugly face much. This was more like dad's ugly face. I looked at Stephanie and she was different also. Her eyes were wild and they volleyed back and forth between mom and me. The warrior was no longer the warrior. She was just like me, but then she wasn't. I wanted to study this part of her I had never seen, but there was no time. Mom was waiting, and I didn't know what to say.

I started to cry. I looked at our mom and sputtered, "She's my big sister and I love her and she can do anything she damn well wants, so leave her alone." Then I ran out of the room and slammed my bedroom door.

And now, here I was sitting in my room with this shoebox open in my lap, staring into the abyss of a new sister again -another one I didn't know. The box was full of strange women's credit cards and driver's licenses -hundreds of them. Where the hell had she gotten them? I lined up some of the cards, studied their faces and checked out their ages. There were blondes, brunettes, redheads, anywhere from 25 to 50 years old. What was I supposed to do with all these anonymous women? And what had Stephanie done with all these women? My mind battled through scenes of tangled bodies all twisted together with my sister somewhere in the middle.

Apparently, Stephanie had multiple, strange faces, just like her vocabulary. She really was some crazy-ass criminal. She had always terrified me before, but now I was in awe of her. I put the box under my bed for a few days and didn't speak with Stephanie or our mother. It didn't seem like either of them noticed. I scrutinized Stephanie at dinner or whenever she was around to see if I could detect some sinister smirk or nervous tic, but she appeared indifferent to any searing gaze I cut into her. How come she didn't notice the box was missing, and why the hell had she kept it around for mom to find if she was such a genius?

I let myself wait until I knew what was expected of a warrior. I knocked on her bedroom door one night and she let me in. I had the box hidden away so she would never find it.

"Well. What the hell do you want?" Stephanie demanded. I had been practicing my lines all day so I wouldn't get tongue-tied in her presence. She did that to me. I raised my arms up for emphasis and thought of Vincent Price on "Dark Shadows" with his quivering, disembodied voice and Sally Field's rendition of "Sybil," the multiple personality all hunched over with puffed out cheeks. "Oh Sybil, what mask do you creep around in? You sinister snatcher of faces–you leftover bone of a sibling. Are you a mass of stolen body parts? Whose costume are you plastered in today? Sybil, Sybil, psycho of a thousand faces, how long can you go on living like this?" I had to stop mid-speech because Stephanie fell backwards on her bed and roared with laughter, rolling back and forth clutching her stomach.

"Oh baby, that was fabulously magnanimous!" Stephanie rolled over snorting and looked up at me. "You really are my sister, aren't you? The rest of them are stuttering zombies, but you? You're a fucking uprising waiting to happen!" She threw herself off the bed and grabbed me in a stranglehold. I started laughing with her. Maybe I was a warrior just like her. She got out a pipe with some weed in it and we sat back on the bed to smoke it. Every time she took an inhale, she'd start giggling again, and then she'd get me started.

I never asked her about all those women's credit cards and driver's licenses. I had done what a true warrior must do. One thing I learned from my family was that secrets were made to be buried. I had taken the box out to

10

the backyard the day before, when no one was around, and got a shovel from the garage. It didn't take long to dig out a shoebox sized burial ground. The year before we had to dig a massive grave for Clem, our dead German Shepherd. I just made sure the hole I dug wasn't next to Clem's.

LEADER OF MEN

My dad was a tall, good-looking man, though his features bore the slight tremor of the frenzied, similar to that strained purposefulness of a dog that has come to the end of its chain, but does not agree. He was waving a butcher knife out in front of himself while he spoke, and with each thrust, the knife, a bit of a yes-man itself, nodded up and down in obvious collusion with dad, who held it, giving an added force to his words that alone they didn't carry. My mom watched dad and the knife equally, but said nothing, though her face, exquisite in its own right, said everything. They stood in front of a wounded tomato that mom had been brutally mutilating before dad had been able to assess the seriousness of the situation and rush in to salvage it from its complete demise. There the tomato sat in front of them, bleeding to death from its right side, a savage testimony to the woman's complete and utter incompetence.

"Wrong," my dad said. "Wrong, wrong, wrong!" He snatched up the knife quickly, calling a halt to this obscene bloodbath. Was it necessary for him to be everywhere at once? Was there nothing that his wife wouldn't destroy if left to her own devices? Mom understood nothing -absolutely useless. Dad held the knife forcefully, and with authority, letting it know immediately that he was in charge now, and it was to do exactly as he said.

"Look," he said. "Look at the knife. See how I hold it?" It was true. In his hand the knife was pointed and dangerous. It was a weapon, an extension of himself. My mom's reddened, shriveled hand had reduced the knife to nothing more than a feeble, clumsy thing that fumbled ridiculously with vegetables, pawing them into a slow and painful death. The blade stuttered and hung its head foolishly, until it became as dull and lifeless as her tongue.

Dad looked over at mom once more. His eyes rolled together in disgusted formation from one side of his head to the other, a trembling final summation of his entire contempt, and without another moment's hesitation he gripped the knife like nothing less than a leader of men, and using swift, competent, ruthless strokes, sliced the remaining portion of the tomato that mom had not been able to deface, whereupon the tomato-eighths, also prepared to show her a lesson she would not soon forget, dropped neatly away from each other and lined themselves up efficiently, cleanly, and precisely -like well-trained little soldiers in uniform red. Dad gave her one more derisive look and swaggered out of the kitchen. Mom stared at the tomato, and then after dad.

"This is your head," she said. Mom slammed the remains of the tomato against the wall and watched them slide artfully, gracefully down to the floor.

MASTER OF THE MASSDOM

My older brother, Nathan, was named after a nun my Irish grandmother knew. Nathan seemed the perfect name for a nun. There were no Sister Cindy's, Scarlett's, or Barbara's for a very specific reason. Sister Garrett was the first nun I met. She had shoulders like a linebacker and was more than capable of kicking my ass or anyone else's that dared to cross her path. She was my first grade teacher. They didn't get less brutal as you moved up the grade school ladder. Sister Bernard was my second grade teacher. She weighed at least 200 pounds, had jowls and sometimes drooled. We called her "Saint Bernard" behind her back.

Nathan was one of those child geniuses. He had taught himself to read when he was three and now read encyclopedias and dictionaries for pure entertainment. He was crammed with miscellaneous facts and elongated words that nobody understood, including the nuns who supposedly taught him. He became an altar boy when he was seven or eight. He could recite the entire mass in Latin after only a few months on the job. Of course, this didn't surprise anyone in our family, including Nathan. There were five of us kids, which was barely a spit of a Catholic family. Most Catholics grouped eight to twelve kids in their brood, but there was a family a few blocks down with twenty-two kids. It took two houses to house the entire dynasty. Nathan was the only one who could name all of them, in chronological order, in less than a minute. Our mom always said their parents won,

14

hands down, first prize for dumbfounding faith in the rhythm method–the only Catholic birth control in existence.

I was four years younger than Nathan. Nobody else I knew did the sort of things my brother conjured up, so I followed him around. He was eccentric by age three, my parents said, when he would steal wrenches and bolts instead of candy or ice cream from the store. He stuck his finger in an outlet to see if it would do what he had heard it would do, and it did. He was working on composing an opera about fish when he was around ten. He sat at the piano for weeks hitting random notes and putting little fishtails up and down his music sheets. It was called, "Dance of the Rainbow Trout," and when the three sisters and a neighbor performed it in our basement it took over an hour to get through. My parents got drunk on martinis. I was only eight at the time, but quite excited to have a few choice singing lines in the piece with my younger sister, Katherine, who was six years old. We wore some of mom's dresses and flitted around singing in high soprano screeches. Nathan cringed and yelled at us whenever we flounced and bellowed, disrupting Stephanie and her friend, who had tons more lyrics to memorize than we did, but Katherine and I knew we were fabulous, floating and twirling. We got hoots and applause from our parents during the only exhibition of "Dance of The Rainbow Trout" that was ever performed in the history of opera as far as I know.

My brother had another exotic pastime that he spent many afternoons working on. We got a dime each week for our allowance and all six of us would march three blocks over to the Woolworth's to find that absolute treasure that only a dime could buy. Nathan always had some plan in mind, but never let me in on it ahead of time. He bought a bag of green army men one week. The next week he bought some paints, and the week after that he bought a chess set. He had a coin collection that he used when he needed extra cash, until Stephanie broke the combination to his lock and took all his rare buffalo nickels and silver dollars up to the candy store and ate up that particular hobby. Nathan was incensed. I'd seen him infuriated only once before, when the same sister locked him in his closet and took off with his new Schwinn stingray for a day. The greatest part of this story, though, was that Nathan planned and set up a sting operation on her. He put some dollar bills in his new safe and waited. He knew it was only a matter of time. He ambushed Stephanie one day when she was on her way up to the candy store. He had dad with him and it took three of us to wrestle her to the ground and get in her pockets to fish out the cash. Nathan was holding a list of the serial numbers of each of those dollars and they matched up number for number with the crumpled bills from her pocket. Unfortunately the sting backfired in Nathan's face. Yes, Stephanie was totally caught red-handed in the act of pilfering Nathan's hard-earned dollars, but dad was horrified that Nathan had been so anal about the whole thing. Nathan was grounded for a whole week, but Stephanie got a lighter sentence because she happened to be a personal favorite of dads. Justice was doled out in irrational spurts that no one could quite decipher.

The good thing was that nothing stopped Nathan, not even his wicked sister. When Nathan had finally gathered all the supplies necessary for his project, he opened up an empty chessboard in the middle of the family room. He cut all kinds of bizarre shapes out of paper with his scissors. He took the cardboard out of dad's new shirts from the cleaners and cut them up as well. Then he painted gold crosses, red streaks, and silver crescents all over them. He made a long table out of cardboard and set it up on the middle of the playing board. He took a long, flat piece of paper with red stripes painted on either end of it and glued it down over the cardboard table. Then he got the army men out. He dressed them one by one. The green plastic figures, some with bayonets and rifles, wore painted paper cutout vestments for popes, bishops, cardinals and priests and spectacular paper hats were glued high on their heads. They were magnificent. He let me sit and watch while he moved the men around the board, holding up paper chalices and chanting in Latin. Stephanie called him a "nerd-ass" from the planet Your-Anus, but he called her a "serpentine lummox" and that shut her up. Stephanie didn't like to be outdone when it came to anything, especially name-stomping. I studied Nathan's moves and waited until I was delegated to be one of the altar boys. That was the hierarchy. Until I learned the basics, I couldn't make my way up the ranks, even if I cherished the bishop's and cardinal's lofty, hand-painted hats.

Nathan would maneuver his characters around on the board in a game of High Mass. There was only one pope who died a horrible death by bayonet at least once a week by the hands of some fiendish cardinal and there were lots of devious cardinals. The cardinals would then all be called in for a secret meeting to find out who was worthy enough to take the pope's exalted place. They were asked questions, such as, "What kind of sacrifices would be made to become the promised Master of the Massdom?" Some said they'd give up food for weeks and only drink holy water. Some would crawl hundreds of miles on their knees in painful pilgrimages. Some would set out into the community to feed the poor and decrepit and, while they were at it, burn down a convent or two full of nuns. (I added that part, and my brother approved.) There were a lot of clandestine gatherings where cardinals decided the fate of various unsavory bishops, while bishops were busy sticking it to the priests, who had their fair share of fallen altar boys who had to be brutally beaten with miniature palms that Nathan had saved from the previous Palm Sunday for showing up late or forgetting their lines. It was a very troubling time for the dioceses, but my brother operated the entire brigade with extremely impressive words in either English or Latin.

When I watched television with Nathan, we didn't actually watch television. There was always a job to be done. Nathan had written up a remarkably technical rating system for the commercials between programs. This would be the only reason we were on the couch without books in front of the television unless, of course, there was a Hitchcock movie or "Twilight Zone" was on. The commercials were rated on artistic individuality, humor, acting ability, engaging dialogue and jingle retention. Each category had five possible responses -sublime, conventional, mediocre, nondescript, and finally, my favorite, fraudulent/degrading. There wasn't much time to get all the answers in before the program was back on because most commercials only lasted a minute or two, and three of them were jammed in between shows, sometimes four, so I was always hunched forward on the couch with my pencil and notebook in hand ready to get to work.

Commercials like Alka-Seltzer's, "Plop, plop, fizz, fizz," always made it to the sublime level in all categories. Women's feminine products or support hosiery were quickly denigrated to fraudulent/degrading. Most commercials, though, were boring and repetitive and fell somewhere in between, but Nathan made watching TV a much more exciting enterprise.

There were downfalls to being the sister of a wunderkind. I never knew what it felt like to win at a board game. Scrabble was a joke. All the dictionary games we knew were concocted from Nathan's head, so, of course, I got creamed. Risk was a washout and Chess was by far the quickest destruction of them all. Nathan had a photographic memory and could count cards, so playing Hearts or Bridge was futile. Sometimes my frustration at losing bordered on hysteria, so I'd either throw the board or cheat in cards. Nathan couldn't figure out why the cards weren't adding up. At least the hands lasted a little longer until he caught on to my game.

I could outrun him though, and beat him at most outside sports, except hockey. Every year he'd ice up the backyard and two or three of his friends would appear to slap a puck around, spit and swear, and generally act like the usual lowbrows in our neighborhood, which disturbed me. Nathan wasn't one of those cretins I knew who played football and barely got C's on his report cards. Nathan built model rockets that actually flew up into the air thousand's of feet. He also took me and my sisters out to bury time-capsules that we put together so future archeologists could find important specimens from our culture like my school photo, my lucky rabbit foot and a scrolled up letter written, "to whom it may concern," stating that I was eight years old, liked to swim, stand on my hands, and my favorite book was "Little Women" by Louisa May Alcott. I tried to give them as much pertinent information as I could. Nathan's was more elaborate. He wrote dates and quotes of various scholars and even left behind an aria that he had composed. We made sure to bury them far from the house in a vacant lot a few blocks down or at the beach. Nathan also built a space capsule in our basement and slept in it on the weekends with some of his friends. It looked like the one on TV except it was made out of cardboard and tinfoil and even had windows cut out and covered over with plastic wrap. No. Nathan was not ordinary like the rest of us. He was an innovator.

His eighth grade teacher, Sister Delbert, was the evilest of all the evil nuns I'd ever come across and older than the bible. She was also maliciously insane. She had a stuffed reindeer she kept up on her desk, whom she talked to and conspired with. The reindeer was named after one of the most sadistic popes in history: Pope Steven VI. This pope had somehow come back from the dead with Sister Delbert to haunt the students through their last year in catholic grade school. Nathan said Sister Delbert and Pope Steven VI had to be the most perfect relationship ever solidified in the history of civilization. Sister Delbert was a stick-pole of a nun with a puckered, emaciated face squeezed into a black and white domed nun's habit. No student dared look directly in to Sister Delbert's rheumy eyes. If one of them did she would smack the kid with a yardstick she used for a cane anywhere on the kid's body she could crack at. The seventh-graders were always praying Sister Delbert would drop dead before they got to their final year.

Sister Delbert doled out punishment according to the agreement made between herself and the reindeer. It was an ongoing one-sided conversation with the reindeer ghost of a pope. She was always going on about the piety and unparalleled bravery of Stephen VI, her reindeer's namesake. "Why he even had the guts to pull those heathens out of the gates of hell and castigate them for their satanistic crimes."

That was apparently one of her standard lines that no one understood, but never questioned. Sister Delbert ranted on as much as she liked about her insane popes and no one said a word. Everyone knew she was crazy and would beat them to a pulp if they opened their traps. There were always at least three bad kids in every class, but in Sister Delbert's class, whoever they were, they kept their mouths shut and saved their hell-raising for recess.

Nathan was the only one in the history of that school that ever stood up and faced Sister Delbert head-on. He wasn't even close to brave or some sort of superhero. It was only that he couldn't stop himself when he heard someone distort what he considered to be facts. Sister Delbert decided to begin the classes' theology lecture that day gurgling on about the various popes and their sanctity. This was one specific subject that Nathan had become increasingly obsessed with. The problem was that they had two completely diverging versions. Sister Delbert's popes were pious and militants of martyrdom, while Nathan's popes were psychotic and made any murderer in Hitchcock's movies look like a saint. Nathans foray into becoming Master of the Massdom of our school happened on just another regular school day during religion class.

"Open your text books to Chapter Six -the popes." Sister Delbert stroked her reindeer to the rustling of pages. "None of you may be aware of the fact that these Popes were descendants of St. Peter and the apostles of Christ, Our Lord, Amen." She narrowed her cloudy eyes and glared at a few of the faces in the front row. "They battled the heathens of paganism to save your pathetic souls. Courageous leaders who lived and died for Christ, so that Catholics could live a life dedicated to the one and only God, our Father. Amen." Sister Delbert crossed herself and bowed her doddering head. She lifted it up sharply and coughed out a laugh. "Any of you slugs want to pass the test I give you next week, you better start memorizing the names of those popes from the first blessed martyr, Pious I, all the way up to present day." She picked up her yardstick and began tapping it on the wood floor. "Life for these noble men was ongoing bloodshed. They didn't let pagans get in the way of Christian morality. Something none of you ignoramuses would know anything about -a cause to live and die for. It takes sacrifice and willpower, and that doesn't mean giving up candy bars for Lent." Sister Delbert snickered, and looked over at her reindeer. "Wouldn't you agree, Pope Steven?" She picked him up and his bells jingled as he nodded his head in absolute accordance.

That's when Nathan stood up. He couldn't keep his mouth shut any longer. I sure wish I'd been in that classroom when he began his sermon the day he decided to educate the class on Sister Delbert's desk mate, Pope Steven VI, but thank God for Nathan's scrupulous memory. I got everything out of him later, word for word I'm sure.

"Some of these pious popes actually had their food served to them out of human skulls. You know, after they'd killed the human they were eating out of. Stephen VI? The one that little reindeer is named after? He actually held a trial to condemn a man who was already dead. He put a corpse on the stand. He would have been locked up in a mental institution if he lived today." The kids in the class just stared at Nathan with admiration, while Sister Delbert whacked her yardstick against the desk to stifle him. Nathan continued. "This corpse was a former pope named Formosus who had already been assassinated. He was a skeleton by the time Pope Steven VI had his body exhumed, dressed him in papal vestments, and set him up on a throne to denounce him. Then they tore off his gowns, cut off three of his fingers and threw him into a river." Some of the students started to giggle. Sister Delbert stood up shaking. Her face was turning a dangerous purple, but Nathan was enjoying his moment in the spotlight. He'd spent eight years in grade school being made fun of for carrying a briefcase to school, reading during recess instead of playing, and always sporting a pocket protector with three pencils hanging out of it, and now, suddenly, his peers were regarding him with reverence.

"And that wasn't the end of the rotting skeleton. Some monk fished him out of the water and buried him again. Pope Sergius, another fanatic, disinterred the skeleton a second time to put him on the stand, found him guilty once again, and then beheaded him. I mean this stuff is so great no one could possibly make it up. You'd never see anything this good on the "Twilight Zone." Nathan was smirking by now with some of the other kids, but sat down quickly when he realized Sister Delbert was stumbling down the aisle toward him. She was slapping the yardstick against the palm of her hand. The rest of the students looked down at their desks as she passed. It was an ugly scene. Nathan had to bend over in front of the class while he got smacked on the ass so many times no one had the stomach to count. He had to sit on a special cushion for a few weeks after Sister Delbert let him have it, but he still said it was worth every whack. Our mother went to the school to place a formal complaint against Sister Delbert, but I doubt mom was the first. Sister Delbert continued to teach eighth grade until she eventually died of some repulsive mouth cancer before I was old enough to get in her class. Some prayers actually did come true.

My brother Nathan became a school legend. I don't think he ever spoke up in class after that, but he did graduate and never had to set foot in a Catholic school again.

I made Nathan tell his story over and over until I had all the details. Whenever I played the Master of the Massdom with my sister, Katherine, from then on, we included a trial with Stephen VI pointing an accusatory finger at Formosus, the army man we'd painted all white with black sockets for his eyes, then we carved off his fingers which took a bit of doing, ripped his paper vestment from his white body, and threw him into a goldfish bowl filled with water that we'd found collecting dust in the basement.

RELIGION

Every night my grandmother limps out of a liquor store with the submissive stoop of the genuflected and the promise of a liturgy to come in a bottle. A radiant, old face with the slight tremor of the merciful, holding a brown paper bag reverently out in front of her with both hands as a priest holds his chalice. And what would be the difference? She has been living, breathing and sucking down the blood of Christ in a lifetime of unparalleled singularity that the clergy can only read about and shamelessly attempt to enact, mouthing their long-winded, incredulous interpretations of the Bible, done up like showgirls in their mawkish vestments.

FAMILY CONFERENCE

I stare out the picture window at a sky. It spreads up there ordinary as buttered bread on a table. Underneath, one block in the neighborhood stares back. The Connollys get into their blue station wagon. No pushing, no fighting, the doors slam shut–they move off down the street. Mr. Hampton mows his lawn and next-door Mrs. Sullivan pulls weeds.

One black fly (Diptera; Muscidae) buzzes up and down the window frame looking for escape, or maybe not. I have a microscope in my room, a pile of dead insects in a cigar box: moths, spiders, flies, bees, a few beetles, two butterflies and one glorious preying mantis.

Fact: One fly strip a week every summer guarantees over a hundred slaughtered. I pull a few live ones off with forceps, place them under the scope, and watch them die.

It reminds me of packaged sausage thawing when I watch the sweat roll down the back of Mrs. Sullivan's fleshy, spider-like varicose-veined legs. Every day this week she's been out roaming her pasture like a cow, doubled over that same scrawny patch of grass, wrenching up mounds of weed clumps and dumping them into a bag. Any passing observer might consider this an honorable pastime for an old lady to overstrain herself in the buckling height of the summer, battling to destroy any foreign substance that rears its parasitic head inside the boundaries of her scoured landscape with a thoroughness comparable to a mother delousing her child's scalp.

But I maintain that you must look closer. Carefully scrutinize this domestic scene so bleakly submerged in the commonplace. It demands much more than the average eye can withstand. The true essence of the person will always reveal itself within the sinister monotony of the habitual.

Truth demands, at the very least, a static eye. Karl von Frisch was one of the masters, discovering that honeybee workers were transmitting detailed information by dance: both the distance to the source of the food and its direction in relation to the sun were reported to the other bees by turning in circles or figure eights. He was a man who dared to barrel his high-powered vision into the droning regularity of the buzzing swarms and do the only thing that separates the truly mystical from the masses. Absolutely nothing, but wait.

I examine Mrs. Sullivan more closely. I reason, first of all, that a front lawn of humble proportions (I measured her lawn one night with a yardstick and a flashlight), twenty feet by twelve feet, must by anyone's calculations come to the end of its weeds fairly soon. It stands to reason that over a sufficient amount of time spent consistently pulling up clumps, day in and day out, Mrs. Sullivan would one day step out of her house to find nothing but dirt.

Twenty dandelions/square foot x 240 square feet = 4,800 dandelions to be picked. Throw in another 1,000 or so miscellaneous weeds that come up every month–ragweed, goat's head, etc. Approximate rate of time allowed for scalping each weed–10 seconds for Mrs. Sullivan's weakest pull. 58,000 seconds can be rounded up to 60,000 seconds to allow for back stretching, wiping of brow and cursing, which calculates to 1,000 minutes or 16 hours, 40 minutes. Round that up to 20 hours to allow for disposing of weeds in a garbage bag, phone-gabbing, neighbor-gabbing, thwarting mosquitoes, and swearing. Mrs. Sullivan has seven days left to finish the task efficiently if she sweats it out less than three hours a day. This, I theorize, will never be the case.

The drone honeybees' sole function is to mate with the queen, yet as soon as one of them mates with her, he dies. The male genitalia evert out of the abdomen on encountering the queen and the resulting shock kills the male. Drones that do not mate are stung to death by the workers and banished from the hive at the onset of winter.

I have been watching for Mrs. Sullivan from my window the last three nights. I contend that long after all the neighbors are snoring and drooling as one, Mrs. Sullivan creeps out in her bathrobe with a headlamp and slides weed clumps back into holes like golf balls. I speculate that Mrs. Sullivan keeps herself occupied at night with this dubious diversion to spare herself from the slovenly clutches of fat man Sullivan, who would have squashed her by now, like he did his first wife, if she really slept with him.

Married people need not have a reasonable reason for unreasonable reasoning. Take Aunt Helen for example. My mom says Aunt Helen detested Uncle Bob when they met. That was right about the time Aunt Helen was turning the ancient age of thirty, which meant she was supposed to tie the bloody knot once and for all according to her screeching mother, but instead of running away like any other right-minded girl, she married the bald, dull-witted Bob.

Most bees will select flowers that are radially symmetrical.

Bumblebees prefer flowers that are vertically symmetrical.

Aunt Helen became a bumblebee in her thirty-first year.

From that wedded day forward Aunt Helen chose to fight her nocturnal battle with creases, wrinkles, and undefined shapes, instead of with Uncle Bob. I stayed overnight at my cousin's more than a few times and sat watching Aunt Helen sweat through entire sleepless nights to create her vertical landscapes of starched perfection. Piles of anything she could get her hands on were ironed. I even saw her take shoelaces out of shoes one night to run them over with the iron.

Megan O'Brien is up on her porch hiding behind one of her raunchy romance novels. Why she wouldn't choose an encyclopedia or an art book to provide a wider expanse to sink behind is beyond me—any book that might lead a passerby to mistake her for a girl with a brain? The truth is she's an imbecile who's never read a book in her life, and so she crouches behind a tawdry paperback ripping away at whatever's left of her fingernails. I've seen those fingers and their stubs of bloody skin with tiny bits of nail barely clinging to them. It won't be long before she has no fingernails left.

When the hell are the Connollys getting back? I look at the empty space where their station wagon was and wonder if they set off for an afternoon of miniature golf and lunch at McDonald's like any decent family ought to on a Saturday afternoon. More likely, they're still circling the neighborhood driving around to the rumbling monotony of their dad torturing them on how to organize their lives before they end up like Rednose Scunner, another of a long line of neighborhood deadbeats who couldn't navigate his way out of his own bed.

I turn back to the Family Conference. We are in session. Dad has already recited the various idiocies of his children and wife, one by one. He usually has a clipboard, but today is working off memory. At some point my older sister, Stephanie, starts shrieking at him. She is the only one who adds anything to these conferences besides dad. Then things begin to move. Dad and Stephanie lunge at each other. It's like one of those wrestling matches on TV. Dad and Stephanie are hunched over, circling, gripping hair from the other's scalp.

"Let go, you bastard!!!" Stephanie wrenches a fistful of hair.

"You psycho bitch!!" Dad grabs her shoulder with his free hand.

"You son of a whore!!" She swings at him and he dodges.

"I'll kill you, you beast," he hisses as they continue to circle.

I survey the room. Mom sits braced on the corner of the couch, rocking back and forth, covering her mouth and clutching her hands, whispering "no" or "stop" every few moments. An open window across from her confiscates whatever sounds she emits. The motoring tirade of Mr. Hampton's lawn mower plows through its riotous business with throttling disregard. I am forced to look directly at mom's lips in order to decipher what she says.

Nathan, my older brother, is on mom's left on the floor in lotus position with his back against the couch, eyes closed, palms up. He has taken to transcendental meditation and claims he has transcended the block more than a few times.

Opposite the couch, a smaller version of the same lumpy beige specimen mocks the room, calling itself a loveseat, with the youngest two saddled close to one another in silence. Katherine, now fourteen, is exploring the boundaries of her hand, biting one cuticle after the other, apparently an advanced stage of sucking the thumb, while Andrea, age twelve, has her arm entwined in Katherine's and is regarding the spectacle with the same numbed out unblinking gaze she has when she watches her Saturday morning cartoons. She is obsessed with cartoons and it's a concern to us all.

Then there's me. Michelle. A sixteen-year-old girl stuck to the window seat like a dead fly on a strip.

"Go ahead, hit me," Stephanie taunts. "Child abuse! I'll call the cops. Scream it for the whole goddamn neighborhood to hear! You'd love that, wouldn't you, you freak!"

Dad coughs out a laugh and jerks her head toward him. Stephanie howls and tries to twist his hand away. They lose their balance and push away from each other, strands of torn hair tight in their fists. Stephanie punches the air while we watch her face turn the remarkable shade of mom's Thursday meatloaf.

"Damn ungrateful brats...this is a goddamn asylum!" Dad lurches around the room waving his arms.

"A damn nuthouse... look at you!!!" Dad stares at each one of us separately.

"No kid talks that way in my house!"

"You're the one who should be locked away, you FUCKER," Stephanie yells, bolting for the staircase.

Dad pulls the back of her t-shirt and swings her down to the rug. He kicks her a few times in the side till she's screaming. Now mom is up running at him and jumps on his back. Her face is chalk-white like all the blood's sucked out of her.

"Monster," she chants over and over till dad forgets about Stephanie and starts swatting back at mom while they spin around. Her legs clamp tightly to him. Her hands attach to his Adams apple.

"Crazed bitch." He struggles to free himself.

"Don't you ever," mom stutters.

Stephanie's bedroom door slams upstairs. No one noticed her slip away. Dad stops circling and stares at the ceiling while mom slowly releases her grip. She slides down his back and falls to her knees. She covers her face with her hands.

The room is silent. One knotted lump on dad's temple pumps between veins like a prisoner behind bars. His frantic eyes search the room as we sink into our shoulders and study our shoes. The haunting idiocy of the lawn mower barrels away outside.

Dad spreads his arms out in a slow, sweeping arc. "Why? Why do you do this to me?" His arms drop to his sides and he searches our vacant faces again.

Passive migration occurs when insects are swept up and carried away, high into the atmosphere, sometimes thousands of feet into the air, and are transported by air currents to new areas.

I watch our house slowly rise up over the ragged stucco of this decrepit little street, over the tan house, the yellow house, the white house. There go the chalk-marked sidewalks and the endless ridicule of coiffed green lawns. There go the shocked upturned faces of Mr. Hampton, Mrs. Sullivan and Megan O'Brien. I watch all the shrinking, parched faces fade away never to be seen again. But as I travel up and over the neighborhood I see the same tan, yellow and white houses on every block, dying and repetitive as their plump square lawns? There is no escape. I let the house sink back into its crumbling frame.

An ambush bug found in Central America kills termites and arranges their dead bodies around the remaining nest of termites, then waits for the others to come out and inspect this camouflage of curiously silent neighbors before it descends on the parade of dupes with deplorable ease.

The human exoskeleton is much thicker than any insect's could ever be. Any number of shifting personas can be detected in an adult in a single day. Depression and hangovers at breakfast turn into uncontrollable rage by lunch, and after a few cocktails by sundown, the adult is delirious and joking by dinner.

The hidden inner tissue of adults is revealed after bottles of scotch, whisky, or beer are opened, and cigarettes and pipes are lit. Cocktail parties are an ideal setting for tracking entire groups of adults getting drunk simultaneously. Those know-it-all blurs of earlier disappear while they reminisce and tell bad jokes.

Each adult holds a sunken continent of memories inside that always come with the accompaniment of wretched sap music. After an hour or so, the group starts singing, and some begin to dance, while their faces redden and they become strangers to the present -to us. The music volume rises up over hovering cigarette smoke. Laughing takes on a maniacal pitch as their reddened lips belt out old sentimental tunes. Some dance hysterically in each other's arms, twirling and throwing each other up in the air. Gross lipstick-stained glasses pile up in sour, sticky little cloisters discarded on end tables around piled ashtrays. It takes patience and a static eye to identify these fools under microscopic focus. Karl von Frisch would have given me the nod as I watch and wait on the stairwell with a notebook in hand, unnoticed by my subjects.

And then the underbelly begins to show itself. Somewhere around midnight the smoky room transforms into a gloomy state. Adults appear dazed and sit closer to each other. Even the music drips into the background. Some of the shakier ones stagger out around this point, using children and babysitters as an excuse to get away. There are the slurred goodbyes and kisses, and we wait for the screen door to slam a few more times before the room settles again.

Now the good stories begin. There exists a whole undersea world of discarded lives that now surface. Adults tell tales of lost loves and exotic places they were going to visit, but never did. Some would have been rich living in huge mansions if they had just taken that computer job, or bought that cheap plot of land that is now a famous ski resort worth millions. One neighbor bypassed a marriage proposal from some poor slob in California, who now owns a vineyard with his name slapped over bottles lining liquor store shelves around the world. Another never took a job in Paris, nor painting classes, nor got that law degree, nor biked through Europe. I keep a running tally of irretrievable dreams. The room gets quiet and more drinks are slugged back. Eyes settle back into rumpled bags and panicked faces grope around in the miserable backwaters of unexplored seas with the low, mocking music of yesterday imprisoning them.

And just when it seems that the room cannot possibly hold its breath a moment longer, it shifts again. Adults grasp for some fragment of rock they can cling to in this ongoing battle for self-preservation of the species. More drinks are passed around, cigarettes lit, and one of the adults announces that her daughter has won first prize in a science fair. Another adult nods her head, filled with the vision of offspring, and soon the room is blathering on about a child's basketball championship, a piano recital, a track meet -swim meets, soccer games, ballet classes, spelling bees, graduations. One or two snatch their purses and search for photos as the driftwood of life never lived floats off beyond the murky waters of the present.

And then the dull, thick exteriors reattach themselves to respective adults as they yawn and get up to leave the party, mumbling good-byes. Their heads are already rattling with tomorrow's agenda.

And as absolute as the rise of another morning's sun, mom and dad are up at the usual time the next day impenetrably dressed in the efficient armor of authority. Mom rubs her temples and searches for aspirin. Dad looks out with bleary, sunken eyes, complaining of his lower back pain. These seem to be the only visible proof of the previous night's excursions.

The day has just begun and they are already railing after us as though all of civilization depended on a pair of matching socks and a combed head.

The drone of the lawn mower has become a dulled lullaby that motors over the inner stirrings of this captive room, while the sharp stench of freshly mowed grass parades in and discharges its flagrant green in random blasts. The fly is still working its way up and down the frame with what looks to be vertical futility.

I read in some magazine that the Declaration of Independence was signed on July 4, 1776, not because that group of arrogant men felt assured of its verbal perfection, but because the horsefly population in Philadelphia was so thick at that specific time of year that the delegates gave up on any further discussion of the document and signed it, fleeing frantically for their respective homes.

Dad sits down in his brown leather recliner with the ottoman pushed off to the side, because, of course, this is a conference. He leans forward, elbows on the rests, hands clasped. The clock on the mantel is burrowed inside its glass house, moving its hands from time to time to keep from appearing suspect. The room is a gallery of dry, muted tongues that wait inside compressed mouths. All eyes prefer the inert reliability of the rug or shoes.

"Children." Dad clears his throat and shakes his head. He laughs and stares down at his hands. He rubs his eye and takes a slow, deep breath.

The lawn mower suddenly sputters off into mechanical death. Everyone but Nathan looks out the window. We wait. The fly is moving down now, buzzing maniacally in a futile battle of will.

"We need to talk to each other! Comm..un..i...," Dad's voice labors the chain of this word while each syllable unlinks from its neighbor. His arms rise up slowly, then drop. A cough fumbles from his throat. He tries to say the word one more time as it shudders from his tongue. He begins to cry, head shaking in his hands, a strong indicator that this conference is about to come to a close.

I look back out the window. Mr. Hampton has just pulled his lawn mower away and is now dragging a hose toward his car. Mrs. Sullivan and Megan O'Brien are back inside.

I watch Mr. Sullivan drag the lumpy bag of decapitated weeds to the trashcan at the back of the house. I have to look into the rate of weed growth. Could Mrs. Sullivan actually sleep with the fat man, and weeds slither up faster than I can calculate?

Mrs. Sullivan is now doing dishes inside. Yellow, plastic gloves are visible from the window across from where I sit. I watch them move back and forth -two yellow agents in a serious battle against filth. I am sure various sponges line the sink at attention, awaiting the final slaughter of any surviving slime that clings to flatware and china for its bacterial life.

I hear our front door slam shut and watch dad hurry down the steps and walk toward our car. Mr. Hampton yells something and laughs. Dad smiles and waves at him, gets into the car and drives off. Mom stands up, smooths out her skirt, smiles blankly at a point above our heads and retreats into the kitchen to cook something. Katherine and Andrea are still pressed together on the loveseat, and Nathan is just starting to flutter his eyelids.

I continue my scan of the street. Mr. O'Brien, Megan's father, is now in his front yard fumbling with the sprinkler. He's about due for his first beer of the day. I check my watch. It's three o'clock. Ellen Rogers clicks quickly past him, late for her afternoon shift at Walmart. She lives in the corner house with her mom and three sisters, never talks about her dad. I found out from Parker, whose brother used to date one of Ellen's sisters, that their dad paid them a surprise visit a couple of years ago and axed in the back door. When the cops found him he was sipping tea, doing the New York Times crossword puzzle, spread out on the couch. Mr. O's screen just slammed. First trip to the fridge.

No one else is out at the moment. Just the same ugly houses decaying in the same ugly row. Flat, green lawns under a flat, blue sky. An oil splatter shines up from the asphalt where the Connolly's station wagon used to sit. It looks to be about the size of a tarantula, round and furry and fat like that. I stare at it long enough to watch it move and change shape. The station wagon isn't back yet. I guess they really went somewhere.

GET IT?

My sister and I are frantic for some kind of thrill every holiday when our cousins finally arrive from the "southside of shallow" as my sister likes to call their neighborhood.

"Listen to me," Stephanie says. "Get one of the cousins alone. Apart from the rest, get it? I've got a plan." I nod and notice that my sister says "get it" all the time after watching too many old gangster flicks with our dad after I've been sent to bed. I pick out the most sedate of the group, Tina, who dislikes Stephanie and I for good reason. I know we inject fear into Aunt Helen, who watches us closely, with a sort of sneer transpiring in the lower regions of her sagging cheeks, as my sister and I say "We're going to go upstairs," and we grab Tina's sweaty hands.

Our mother shakes her finger at us, but we just smile and wave. "Come on, Tina." We climb the stairs slowly, and push the door open to the attic. Tina looks pale, but her reflexes keep her moving forward. Stephanie checks down the hall before closing the door, to make sure no one is following. She tells Tina to sit down. We form a circle on the rug in this musty, prison-like room. Stephanie reaches behind the couch and pulls out a bottle of Jagermeister. She stole the bottle from dad's "shop" as he likes to call it. That's where he keeps his liquor supply, hidden inside his power tool cabinet in the basement where he sits and gets soused on the weekends.

One by one, Stephanie lines up three tall glasses already filled up to the length of a new pencil. She measures them to show us that each glass has exactly the same amount. "Okay now, focus both of you." She stares at Tina and smiles. "This will happen only once, get it? There's that damn "get it" again.

"This is the method, Tina," Stephanie continues. "The thrice of ice, that's what I'll call us. Adventurers delving into the recesses of lore to suck down our absinthe, go down together." Tina and I just stare at Stephanie. I was used to her back-ass language, but Tina sat up a bit straighter and smiled when she should have been terrified.

"We're going to chug down a glass of this black elixir when I say go, and the one who blasts it down the fastest is in for an explosive surprise!" She never shares what that surprise might be, but it doesn't matter. Tina is ready to follow us anywhere.

"Also good practice for the minors, get it?" Tina looks wary, but nods her head. Stephanie had already set up the glasses earlier. She filled two of the glasses with coke and a shot of Jager, but the final glass that sat in front of Tina was straight up Jagermeister. I was getting sick just thinking about shooting back that black lagoon.

"On the count of three we all go for it. One." Tina picks up her glass. "Two." Her mouth is starting to pucker up. "Three! Down the hatch my chicky mates!"

Our heads tilt and we start to empty our glasses. Burning bubbles start burping out of me, but I am intently peering over my glass at Tina's face. As she swallows down the deadly liquid her skin turns into a rainbow of color, moving from red to an enchanted sort of dead-body blue. When we finally set our glasses down Tina's eyes are like that roller coaster ride I took last summer at the carnival. They are careening wheels rolling around in her head. I can make out laughing and chattering voices downstairs. Stephanie and I look at each other. We hear footsteps slowly making their way up the stairs.

"Oh, shit," I screech as Tina suddenly projectiles vomit on to her shoes, her new dress and the white couch that now showcases a brown Jagermeister, pinwheel-stain on it.

The noxious creak of the door spits it open, and my sister and I look up into Aunt Helen's ominous eyes as her ashen daughter wretches in front of us, on her hands and knees.

DOMESTIC APPARITION

A phantom in life can become a ghost. I had my own paint-by-number vision of Aunt Helen. She was a thick slab of beige that looked like my mom, except not outlined. She came to visit without our cousins once. She and mom talked about the weather. They talked about their kids. Their eyes jumped around like crickets in a paper bag. My Aunt had hair wig-piled on her head. Sometimes she stopped eye-flailing and stared at the carpet. Her swaddled legs sandwiched themselves in pantyhose. Her hands were shuddering bodies clutching each other and she never smiled. I wanted to hug her hell away. I wanted to unhinge her skull and see what it was that kept her alive. Sometimes she tugged and pulled her long, brown skirt down over knees as though there were something under there she didn't want to know. She sniffed before she spoke, rustled words and looked troubled. I deadlocked her until I could barely see her. Mom, pale and empty, embraced her before she left. Aunt Helen's slackened face stumbled around itself. She groped for my hand. Her dry fingers were brittle-cold. I narrowed my eyes until she was a blur of washed out bone swallowed up by the world. "Mom," I said, as I watched her leave. "Don't let her go." Mom looked vacant and smiled at the door.

*   *   *   *

An annihilating scream shook with the beat of a death rattle. It came from downstairs. It was mom. I'd never heard her scream. She was a brow-beaten housewife who dad terrorized into a breath of herself. Her owl eyes rarely blinked anymore. I descend. Maybe she jumped, or better yet, plunged a kitchen knife through dad's gut. Step by step. Whimpering echoed from her room. I pushed the door open and it creaked, just like in the movies. She was rocking, teetering on the edge of the bed. Her marble eyes stared into a place I was afraid I would someday go. "Mom?" The phone is off the hook in her lap. "Mom?" The phone started beeping and mom was moaning. She looked at the wall and whispered to herself, "My Helen, my baby sister is dead. She killed herself."

GARBAGE PICKER OF MEMORY
Letter from Aunt Rita

Dear Michelle,

You asked me to write my story. Here it is as I see it today. But don't forget, memory is a marauder. Tomorrow everything changes.

I, too, am a murderer. I did not kill by violence or bloody means. My daughter, Beth, was twenty. Yes, it was true that no one saw me cry, not even at the funeral, but why would tears travel in public streams when what we are given to see of the world's bodies of water are nothing more than flat blue blots on paper or shorelines that whisper a mere spittle spray of the vast rivers, lakes, oceans and seas? The doctors found malignant tumors under Beth's right arm, which they cut out. Then they viciously attacked her armpit with radiation and chemotherapy. But I knew those lumps would take up residence and destroy other parts of her body instead, because they were lumps in my throat that I'd swallowed my entire life, contracted from my mother who'd carried them like a totem pole in her spine, until one day she'd sat down in a chair, never to rise again. One long continuous wailing NO that unleashed its deadly poison from out of me into the silent chambers of my daughter's blood.

You see, I have always been a coward. It is only at night in my bed, in my dreams, that I have fought and screamed, kicked and swore, the dry-eyed arrested battles of the nocturnal, which served to raise me, like a tree, with the sun.

I married your Uncle Sherman, blinded by a love that turned out to be a corrective astigmatism. We chose not to see each other clearly until after we'd crossed the threshold. He came to detest me as quickly as I did him. Our duet played out like soup slurped from a spoon. I sucked in his abuse and commandments and swallowed them along with my fear, my tongue and myself.

I'd hear over and over, "Why don't you get off your fat ass and do something, Rita?" When I hardly had an ass to speak of.

"Look at this pig-sty! How can we possibly invite anyone into this house?"

I would sing that song in my head to drown him out. "Hush little baby, don't you cry. Mama's going to buy you a piece of pie." I made up my own lyrics. I could never remember them, but one time when I got to the "Momma's going to buy you a mocking bird" part, this blue bird just appeared on the windowsill.

Sherman didn't see it. He was too busy ranting, "What the hell do you do all day? I work all goddamn day… blah, blah, blah."

There it was, blue as sky and magnificent. I swear it looked right inside me and I was transfixed. I thought for the first time that I could escape. Start a whole new life somewhere far away, where no one knew me. I'll never forget that bird. As soon as it flew off, I felt rage building up inside me and I stared at Sherman's globular, reddened face blithering on in front of me and almost spit in it. I hated Sherman, but I was afraid. He'd hit me a few times. My daughter, Beth was the only thing that gushed out of me from this coupled inferno. She grew up watching and waiting for the volcano bubbling in my throat to erupt, but it never did.

Instead it ruptured out of Beth in short, fevered spurts of hatred toward me when her father was out. "All you do is pick up and cook for that asshole. You're nothing but his slave. He doesn't give a damn about you!"

She feared her father's chronic rage as much as I, knowing it could turn on her as quickly as he did on me. She walked in one time when Sherman had me up against the living-room wall by my throat.

Sherman was a horror film. I'd come home and test the atmosphere in the room, searching for undertones of rage in his bone-chilling stare. His fabricated face, pliable in its chilling meteorological leaps and depths ravaged over his features like a typhoon blasting through a village built on sticks. He loved his goddamn whiskey.

Sometimes the churning volcano threatened to swallow Beth up. When she was a teenager she discovered it could be tempered and held beneath the surface with liquor and pills, leaving her with a tongue as fat as a bible and eyes as vacant as glass. She slammed and locked her door every

49

night, communicating what her thickened tongue did not, until the day she discovered those lumps of mine lodged under her arm in a tight little ghetto of clustered family heirlooms.

How was she murdered? Like memory. A car crash would have proved no more sudden than her prolonged illness, where the deathbed was just another vehicle that bore the domestic appearance of the everyday.

I stationed myself by my daughter's bed, feeding her, changing her and cleaning up the scattered eruptions of fluids that drained from her body while the deadly settlements of cancer spread themselves out for two long years inside her.

Clocked revolutions of meals, bathing, dressing, laundry and medications must have been seen by the world as loving acts by a devoted mother, but these were my weapons.

Clean sheets were snapped down to cover her, tucked in with fingers raw with apology, sealing her in, tight as a drum in a family compression that feet would never be strong enough to kick out of.

Pillows, pounded and puffed up, bore the bruises never raised from my sagging cheeks of repression.

Milkshakes, whipped out of life's resignation, were my pride sucked by my daughter in lumps through a straw.

The days moved on, taking her from me until one day I stood before a corpse. My hands, unconvinced, groped their way desperately around her sheets, creasing and tucking in disbelief.

"Rita, I'm your sister. Talk to me. Please."

"I've got all these people over, Lucy. I've got to feed them. I've always hated parties when there's never enough food to go around, haven't you? Would make us look cheap, and I won't have it." I picked up a tray of meatballs and started to make my way out of the kitchen, past Lucy, with that empty stare I now owned.

"Rita, I'm dying along with you, here! I loved Beth like she was one of my daughters. You've held up that front long enough." Lucy grabbed me by the shoulders. Your mother could be forceful when she needed to.

"Forget the goddamn food and guests. This is your daughter's goddamn funeral and haven't we been through enough!" I remember Lucy started to cry. "We already lost our baby sister, Helen! It's too much to lose, Rita!"

"You did everything for Beth, Rita. You were always so strong. She was lucky to have you for a mother." Lucy put her arms out to hug me, and you know what I did? I pushed past her with that damn tray in my hand.

"It's okay, Lucy. I'll be right back." I patted Lucy on the head like I was petting a dog. "Food's getting cold." And that was it. I slipped out of the kitchen with your mother crying and we never spoke of it again.

It was said that my silence became impossible to talk over. It carried the wailing hands and tearing hair of a multitude locked up inside it. They called it shock, and then it was depression–this grief where words have always been stones, and the body, a traitor–and so voltage with its immediate answer to dark rooms was the only prescription to tear up these crypts. A shock for a shock, though none of the doctors, nurses, my husband or my sister, your mother, knew that while they electrocuted my brain, attacking and destroying synapses, assuring each other that these violent convulsions were necessary to successfully implode all disruptive memory into irretrievable waters, this vision of Beth's murder was doubled up in ten shrieking digits, five on either side of me that clutched each other tightly, crouching in terror inside my two bloodless fists.

And the other murderer? You think it was Helen, right? No. Helen may have killed herself, but she didn't linger through the pain. It was Lucy, mother to all you heathens. You never got to know what a genius she was. Now, that was a crime. She taught herself to read and devoured every book she could get her hands on.

"What you reading now, Lucy?" I asked, tapping my foot on the stack of books leaning against the couch Lucy was stretched out on.

"Gone With the Wind," said Lucy, without looking up.

"But that's a movie, stupid. We already saw it," I said, wanting Lucy to play some hopscotch with me outside."

Lucy put her massive book down and rolled her eyes at me. "It was a book long before it became a movie, stupid." She picked up the book. "And by the way, it's by a woman author, and that's what I'm going to be someday."

I was jealous that Lucy had something I didn't have. Ambition. I couldn't imagine what I'd be. I just wanted to get outside and play.

The sick part was that Lucy never found a place to feed that knowledge. It was the fifties and everyone was getting married. Your mom dropped out of school and married Peter with his perfect teeth and reliable job. None of us knew what kind of idiots we got married to, until after we tied that deadbolt of a knot. Your father, Peter, was just like the rest of them, riding your mother like a racehorse each night until she was rotting in a suburb with five screaming kids.

Evil clutters through the species and no one with an eye toward humanity could keep from tripping over it for long. Humans will destroy each other under the guise of lust, religion, nation, possessions or boredom, when it really goes no further than the length of an arm or the downward slope of the spine. I watched a man cross a street and viciously beat another guy with a lead pipe, with nothing more than a few grimaces and some staggered posturing exchanged. Not a word passed between them. If you forget for a minute that you're a mammal, then you had better watch your back.

I wish I'd taken a stick to Sherman. Hell, even Peter, your father. But no, that would have been the sane thing to do.

Lucy and I slaughtered ourselves instead with the slow, agonizing paper cuts of day-to-day existence. Lucy wanted to be a writer, but there she was for five damn years, swollen up like the world's pride. She could have been great. She put pen to page for a few years in college and then gave up on both when she got married. All five of you kids blame Peter for Lucy's depression, but your mother didn't fight for her life. Neither did I.

One day, when you were a pack of toddlers crying for something, Lucy just started screaming along with you.

"Rita?"

"Peter, are you okay?"

"It's Lucy. She's lost it! I mean really gone! She's howling like a raving maniac and I can't stop her. Can you get over here, please!"

I could hear Lucy and you kids all railing away together in the background.

"Help me, Rita, I can't do this."

And so, I came over, of course, and took care of you kids. Your mother had lost it. Lucy carried on for seven days and seven nights, no matter what Peter and I said. I have to say I got some pleasure from Lucy screaming on and on for a whole week. It meant she still had life in her. She wasn't going to kill herself like Helen did.

She was a psychotic mess, though. She was in the psych ward for six weeks. I know. I was her only visitor. But once she was sent back home, we lost touch. I had my own life to work out. Sherman and I barely spoke to each other, but carried on with the usual tasks in what looked to the world to be a civil marriage. He screamed at me, but only in the privacy of our home. He kept working and brought in the money, but whatever love had once been between us was barely a flicker of a memory now.

Whenever I came to visit, which wasn't often, your mother, Lucy, sat on the lawn chair out on your porch while you kids were at school and stared at the same trees, pedestrians, and passing cars. Her face was bland. The sound of footsteps frightened her. She never looked toward them. Her features froze and her head trembled until they passed. I bit my nails. I know I didn't come to visit much, but our love for each other had survived much worse.

We were two middle-aged women then, sitting up on a porch. In summer you would not be able to pass more than a few streets without spotting a pair of us. Little did we shift our direction as we would the world of words. Lucy used to love to talk when we were young and now she barely spoke.

I did not scream, nor beat Sherman, nor throw dishes when Beth died, though for this there would have been no penalty. Everyone watched instead, while I did nothing. I found no respite from the piteous, elongated faces with their eyebrows up, waiting for what? What had been a whole life of one thing suddenly became another. Lucy said I was in shock for three months, and then it was depression, and what was different? The house was vacuumed and meals were made. I ran errands and bought groceries. There wasn't a light bulb burned out in the house. Sherman continued to work. He may have wailed in public, I don't know, but no one followed him around. He was under no suspicion. This non-performance of mine proved as lethal as Lucy's over-performance, and yet there were no dramatic battles here and no one dragged me off the stage. My sister and husband had said, "look, maybe..." and then I found myself sitting three times a week with a psychiatrist who smiled and called shock therapy a "clearing out." I smiled back, like an imbecile, and said, "Nobody would mind if they opened the drapes a little wider and lightened up the room." Lucy held my hand while my husband signed papers. My brain was electrocuted for three weeks and I was bathed and fed.

Your mother's story was different, but the same. Your father swore he could feel the accusations of the people he passed in cars when he raced his hysterical wife to the hospital. They probably assumed he was a wife-beater or a kidnapper. One swift injection of a tranquilizer by an able nurse and the perverse cradle of a straitjacket delivered, within moments, an abrupt salvation of silence and the return of the Lucy that your father, Peter, had married, but not before he'd signed some papers as well.

Lucy was put out to pasture for four weeks of electrocution and puddled meals. She liked to talk in those days. She told me about Peter's mistress. She'd overheard him lusting on the phone one night with a younger woman. It was some girl he'd met somewhere or another. It didn't matter. Their marriage had been over for a while. It's just that Lucy hadn't seen it coming. She had actually trusted the image of marriage, even though Peter confessed to me one day that they hadn't had sex in years.

* * * *

I have found in life that there is never one set version of history, just as there are multitudes of roads that lead to the same destination. Lucy screamed and I did not, and yet we ended up in the same place: the psych ward getting shock therapy. Our sister, Helen, took the fast track out. Peter may have left his wife behind to fend for herself and the children, but there are certainly many men that have paved that particular road.

They say they took some of my memory from me when I had electric shock therapy, but what of it? Memory is just another collection that we store in our pockets of brains like we would on a shelf.

* * * *

So, now I live alone. I'm an old lady and Sherman is dead. You know that. What you probably don't know is that I spend most of my time riding buses these days. I have traveled the city from line to line with a transfer and followed the threads of history as they are picked up at one corner and dropped off at another. Some of the blindest, old women I know have knitted the rattiest snarls of yarn into masterful canvases of scarves and sweaters, so why shouldn't I be capable of bleeding together a few fragmented stories out of the massive downpour of discarded babble that never ceases. With my monthly bus pass I follow an endless trail of saliva from stranger's mouths–set my bucket under it, so to speak, and guess what I find? Murderers in every one of them.

I call myself the garbage picker of memory. It situates me with the species. History is a massive web of stories that have been locked up in textbooks and museums, lined up single file by chronology.

Civilization, colonization, war, famine, and all those kingdoms march before you, yet you need only put your ear up close to any of those textbooks to hear the silent screams of millions buried alive by that print. They reach out from those iron bars of words, screaming and pounding in futile agitation from the buried cells of the past, and yet look at these ridiculous beasts parading their costumes and stuffed with their facts that call themselves history when they are no more representative of the truth than the sacred beasts we line up on our own private mantels in the guise of memory.

Are we not all trash collectors of the past? Time and memory can only be murdered by fear. We destroyed our younger selves, but to hell with those old photographs. We have all found a way to create our own beginnings and endings to make up for the life the world never gave us. Just get on the next bus and listen. Helen and Beth are dead, but they come alive every time I speak or write. Now, I open my damn mouth and say whatever the hell I feel. I guess you already got that from this letter.

* * * *

So, how do I end this? With my sisters and I, of course. Lucy, Helen and I have come to an understanding. Lucy lets me write the stories she never did, especially the stories of Helen and Beth. I sit next to Lucy and read them when I visit. Lucy listens and laughs and I can feel the ghosts of Helen and Beth chuckling along with us. That is more than enough.

Two, old women sitting up on a porch. In summer you won't pass more than a few streets without spotting a pair of us. We are as dismissed and as old as the trees, but we still hold an ocean of history inside us. Believe me.

BRENDA STANTONOPOLIS

It wasn't her guts I hated. It was other parts of her anatomy I despised. Sparkling, ivory teeth spread out across her face like piano keys plastered beneath a witless pair of shimmering lips. I would stare at her flat incisors while she blustered on about something inane and fantasize blacking out a few of them with my fists to complete the keyboard. I did take a black marker to her high school yearbook photo, but that satisfaction was merely momentary, for I knew that that was all I was capable of. She was an amazon with incredible clout. I was long bones with a bit of meat on me in all the wrong places. Most of the time I tried to stay clear of her.

The only body parts that pushed out ahead of her teeth were her boobs. They torched out of her chest like two upended lampshades with little balls on the ends where her nipples saluted.

She spent hours lying out in the sun, summer or winter, to keep her skin a malted shade of bronze and she stood almost six feet tall with her shoulders and back permanently arched to provide an ample view of the panorama of her breasts.

These were the years of fluffy pastel sweaters, hip-hugger bell-bottoms, wedged heels and Farrah Fawcett fan-feathered bangs. Brenda Stantonopolis took to all of it with unimaginative gusto. She was an icon of an era, at least within the limited circumference of her brain and the limited blocks of our neighborhood.

Everything on her was oversized–big teeth, big head, big body, and big mouth. The first time I saw her throw back her feathered head and bray I knew I was in the presence of someone unforgettable. She was impossible to ignore. She went to every party, went after every guy I did and got him, and attended the same high school, so I ran into her everywhere. I have to admit I was in awe of her success. Brenda got what Brenda wanted.

Stantonopolis and I had come to an understanding, even if it was a shallow one. We were bound together through our high school years, not by loyalty, friendship or respect for one another, but by something much deeper and long lasting: the drugs. We had a common goal. We had to work the same neighborhood to find pot, hash oil, mushrooms and acid, and the neighborhood was far from extensive.

Another despicable component of Brenda was her nerve. I'm not aware of where that nerve was located in her body but I knew it was much bigger than her boobs or her teeth. It was massive enough to plague my neurotransmitters into uncharted areas of my being. She had the nerve to try and take me down in order to save her hugely, prominent ass.

* * * *

One day I was forced to come to terms with Brenda. Nothing seemed out of the ordinary on this Saturday afternoon around five o'clock. I had just left the house after the usual argument with my mom about curfew. She said, "Eleven." I said, "One." She said, "Eleven-thirty." I said "Twelve-thirty." I don't think we resolved it. I left anyway. My dad was the only person who drove a car in our family. He said when any of us got a job and saved some cash to buy our own car, then we could drive. Until that time I was forced to take the bus over to Dolores Delgado's house. She had a beat-up, dark blue Camaro with an eight-track tape player. We'd drive around and get stoned listening to "The Low Spark of High-Heeled Boys" on weekend afternoons before we met up with everyone at the beach as soon as it got dark.

* * * *

Here's how it went according to my sister and my mom. The phone rang at my house after I had left. My older sister picked it up. It was a police officer calling to speak with mother. Mom said, "What the hell?" to my sister before reaching for the phone. "Hello, this is Mrs. Lucy Trenton."

"Hello, Mrs. Trenton. Sorry to bother you, but it seems we've got your daughter, Michelle, here with us at the station on Montgomery Boulevard and Clemens St. We need you to come and retrieve her," said the officer.

My mother was in shock. "What? Michelle? She just left about a half an hour ago. What in God's name could she possibly have done in that amount of time?"

There was a pause before the officer continued. "She was picked up for indecent exposure."

My mother told me later about the strange images battling through her brain. She saw me flashing some poor guy on the street, but I barely had anything to flash so she was considering what else I could have done. "What do you mean indecent exposure? What could she have shown to the world in less than a half an hour?" mom stammered, worrying about my mental health.

The officer seemed to be reading from some report when he replied. "She was picked up at 5:30 on the afternoon of October 23rd. The call came in at 5:15. Michelle Trenton was found squatting in the Clayton's backyard with her pants down, excreting on to their lawn. She was intoxicated and we have cause to believe she was under the influence of something other than alcohol as well. A blood test has been taken and we're waiting for the results. There were reports by the policeman who picked her up that she was not alone, but the subjects ran off when they spotted the squad car. Miss Trenton was too disoriented to flee the scene. She was belligerent and verbally abusive to the policeman. We have her in custody and will release her to you on two conditions. You need to bring one hundred dollars in cash to post bail and Michelle must see a counselor for alcohol and substance abuse for a minimum of six weeks."

My mom was stunned. "Are you sure you have the right girl? I mean this seems a bit deranged, if not impossible, for a sober girl to leave the house less than a half-hour ago and suddenly a policeman finds her pooping like a dog in someone's yard completely soused?"

"She had no identification on her, but gave us your name as her mother and your phone number and address. Do you reside at 1342 Rosemont St.?" The officer waited for her reply.

"Well, yes, but this seems beyond the scope of sanity." I'm sure my mother was now whispering into the phone.

"I'm sorry, Mrs. Trenton. Like I said, we'll have her here at the station and will wait for your arrival. Just ask for Officer Blake at the front desk. See you shortly. Goodbye." The officer hung up the phone.

I can only imagine the depth of hell mom was in as she took the hundred dollars out of her wallet she hid in one of the shoes in her closet that I periodically pilfered from, and made that trip to the station. Mom didn't drive either, so she and my sister walked the six blocks up to the corner, waited for a bus and then rode it down to the station, which was at least forty-five minutes away. My sister said mom was in a scary state, all pale with her mouth as thin as a dime and white knuckles clamped over the purse in her lap. She didn't say anything the entire trip. When they finally got to the station mom quietly asked for Officer Blake.

"I'm Mrs. Trenton. I'm here to pick up my daughter, Michelle."

"Yes, Mrs. Trenton. Right this way," said the cop.

Mom didn't say another word. She and my sister followed the cop to an office in the back. When he opened the door, the room was empty. A chubby woman cop came back from somewhere with a frantic look on her face.

"She's gone! We let her go to the bathroom and somehow she escaped. We just put an all-point bulletin out on her. Her photo was given to some of the officers here before they left and a description was given to the rest of the officer's already on patrol with her address. She might be on her way home."

The man cop looked at the woman cop with disgust and turned to our mother. "I'm so sorry, Mrs. Trenton."

"I want to see that photo you took of her," mom said. Now, that was smart. My mom didn't usually ask authority figures for anything. She usually waited for them to make the demands.

The cop left them in the empty office for a few minutes. My sister said a few nasty things about me, but mom didn't respond. Her mouth remained paper-thin, so my sister shut up. The cop finally returned with those three-way- placard-held-to-the-chest photos and handed them over to my mom. She stared at the photos in horror. My sister looked over her shoulder.

"That's not Michelle. That's her slut-backed friend, Brenda Stantonopolis," my sister said.

"Do you have any photos of your daughter, Michelle with you," asked the officer? My mom said she had five kids who were no longer babies, so why on earth would she carry a photo of any of them? "That's not my daughter. Now, I expect you to straighten this out, and straighten it out quick! I don't know this Brenda's home phone or address, but I'm sure you can find it in the phonebook. My daughter would never have done something like this! Call that girl's parents and get them down here. I'm not leaving until I have a word with them." My mother clutched her purse in her lap and stared ahead until the officer left the room.

The cops made calls and changed all reports. Mr. Stantonopolis appeared at some point shortly thereafter. He had a car and could drive, unlike my mother. My sister said he looked mean as hell and had one of those pencil-curl moustaches and spoke with a thick Greek accent. She said he was cursing in Greek when he saw those photos of his daughter. His face turned beastly red. My sister said she was sure that when he got his hands on Brenda he was going to beat the crap out of her.

"Mrs. Troonton, I can't tell you how very, very sorry I am for trouble my filthy, trash girl cause you. She will punish for this. She will pay for pain she cursed on you and your family. You count for this on me." He raised a shaky finger with clenched teeth.

My mother and sister got up after the officer apologized and left. "Find Michelle when we get home," mom directed my sister. The ride back on the bus was much less tense, but still silent. My sister told me I owed her big time for this complete waste of a day. She didn't bring up our mom.

*   *   *   *

Every Friday and Saturday night the cops chased my friends and me from one spot to the next, though we never changed our course. First stop was always Bedford Beach. A group of about twenty of us would park cars and drink beer. Sal Posconi had graduated high school after seven years and now had a job as a butcher. He got paid on Fridays, so he'd pull up in his truck with a keg tapped and ready to go. The drugs were less reliable. There was usually some pot and sometimes hash oil, but on rare occasions somebody would come along with some windowpane, which were tiny squares of paper, each with a drop of acid on it. This always made the gatherings more interesting. Brenda actually had some worthwhile, if not peculiar, skills. She claimed, when on acid, that she could see farts. "There's one," she'd say and point to someone's ass in the group. "There's another, and another," and believe me this became quite entertaining for the few of us who were privy to her particular talent. We would narrow our eyes and stare at the ass she had just pointed to and wait to see if some kind of ethereal mist snaked out of it. One girl thought she spotted what was described as one flaming shot rocketing out of some guy's posterior, but that was her only alleged sighting. Brenda secured the gift.

Brenda also knew a lot more about sex than the rest of us. We were a circle of girls that surrounded her like vultures pecking at a carcass whenever she brought up the subject. My first sexual encounter didn't size up to anything that came out of her mouth. I was blasted drunk and lay like a corpse underneath Sheldon Feldway, who looked like he was doing push-ups on top of me, up and down, up and down, until he finally sputtered one last time, pulled out of me and collapsed next to me like a cadaver. I had no idea I was supposed to spiral around and make interesting sounds. Now that I had met Brenda and listened intently to her tales I knew that it was possible for a girl to ride anybody she dared to, like Sheldon had, and actually enjoy it. That was a revelation, but I was sure I had a long way to go before I could transport this knowledge into practice.

Brenda not only saw farts, but had imprinted in her brain almost every penis in the group scattered around us and we learned that each one had it's own particular slant. Kevin Coleman's was the size of her index finger and just as thin, Sal's was more like an Italian sausage with balls the size of billiards, while Chuck Pilcher, the shortest guy in the group, had one that hung between his legs like a foot long hotdog. The Cullen brothers weren't circumcised and their schlongs reminded her of rolled up pancakes. Chester Patterson's leaned to the left and surprisingly Sheldon Feldway's leaned to the right. I hadn't noticed his penis. I was too busy trying not to feel like the nail under a pounding hammer when we did it.

Brenda certainly had her share of information that did not go unnoticed, but most of the time, especially when I was high, I would watch her unhinged jaw see-saw back and forth non-stop, with those glow-in-the-dark teeth gnawing at words and nausea would well up inside me. I'd walk away. There was only so much of Stantonopolis I could take.

* * * *

By the time all this had transpired with my mother and sister in another part of the city it was almost dark and Dolores and I had just scored some green buds from this older guy we'd met at the beach one day. He always had the best pot and Dolores had some cash. We got back in the Camaro and I stuck in the eight-track tape of Steve Miller's Band and we were on our way to Bedford beach. My sister would know exactly where to find me, but it would take her longer to get there. After the long bus ride home, she had to hop on her bike and trek it down another half-hour to the beach. Dolores and I picked up Marsha and Jackie on the way over, getting more stoned the closer we got to our destination. There was already a group assembled when we arrived. It usually started out with the girls congregating in tight little circles and the guys surrounding Sal's truck, each of them with one hand in a jean pocket and another holding a plastic cup. We said hi to some of the guys and Sal filled up a beer for each of us. We made our way over to the girls.

69

Brenda was holding court as usual. There were about five of them tucked in close and when they saw us approaching they started laughing. I had a good buzz by then, but now I was getting paranoid. They all seemed to be staring at me. "What's up," I whispered to Dolores, but her glazed eyes told me that she didn't even hear me. I could see Brenda's teeth radiating in the dark.

"Hey," Brenda said when we joined them. She took a long swig from her cup and I could see that she was way ahead of the rest of us. Mascara caked under her fat, closely-knit red eyes. She could barely keep them open. Her mouth and teeth took up most of her face.

"Hey Michelle, what a story I got for you," slurred Brenda. All of them started laughing again and my heart pounded. "You talked to your mom lately?" she asked.

What the hell did that mean? "No," I smiled, trying to act casual. "You talked to yours?"

Her eyes squinted at me, wondering if I already knew something. "What does that mean?" she asked, swaying back on her heels. She was wasted.

"What?" I asked.

"Listen," Brenda spat at me. I noticed everyone was silent around us. More paranoia set in. My hands began to shake. I took long gulps from my beer.

"I got in some trouble today. Sal and Jake and Laurie all got away from the cops, but they got me, those fuckers." Brenda let the word "fuckers" slide through too many syllables.

"What happened," I asked? Everyone in the captive group was concentrating now.

"Can you believe it," she threw back her head and snickered. "They got me for shitting in someone's yard."

"No way," came out of various mouths and we were all laughing again.

"No fucking way."

"Yeah, well they called it Ndecent 'sposure." Brenda couldn't get out the 'ex' part of the word. I thought this was hysterical. The picture of her with pants at her ankles crouched over grimacing on someone's lawn taking a shit was beyond rich. The image was just too beautiful. Brenda Stantonopolis caught with her pants down, but not in the usual act. We were all roaring by now.

"What happened next," Dolores yelled or squealed or both.

"They put handcuffs on me. Can you believe that bullshit? I was still hoping I could make a run for it, but the bastard stuffed me into the squad car. Not before I kicked him a few times and let him know what I thought of him, the asshole." She staggered back a few steps and snorted. "He kept asking me my name. No way I was giving him my real name. Hell, no! My dad would fucking kill me if he found out." She looked in my direction. "But, you know what I finally told that cop?" We were all waiting. Brenda looked directly at me through her blackened slits. "I told him my name was Michelle Trenton." She started to laugh. "That's what I told him."

I stared at her in disbelief. I don't know what kind of mask my face took on when everyone looked my way.

"Had to, Michelle. My dad would've killed me, you know. Your parents are so cool. Member one night your mom let us smoke pot in your attic? I'd be dead before I could do that in my house. Beaten to death!" Brenda kept her eye sockets level with mine. "Anyway, it's over now. Nothing's happened, see?" She raised her hands up and shrugged. Some hideous gurgle came out of her before she burped.

I grabbed Dolores's cup because mine was empty and threw it in Brenda's face. Everyone backed away while Brenda rubbed at her soaked face with her jacket sleeve. "You bitch," she spit out.

I stared at Brenda in amazement. That nerve of hers must have been longer than both her intestines combined. I think I opened my mouth, but nothing came out.

Somebody yelled that the cops were coming and everyone started running for cars. Two squad cars pulled up instead of one, blocking the exit to the beach. They usually pulled out a megaphone and yelled for us to move along and we always did.

I was sitting in Dolores's Camaro. She was busy masticating the remainder of our pot stash. I was slamming my fists against the dashboard shouting out random threats. Brenda was in Sal Posconi's truck saddled up next to him. She'd been doing him exclusively for a while. He was the only guy with a job. She loved to strut around school with some new piece of cheap jewelry around her wrist or her neck that he'd bought her, as if anybody cared.

A cop got out of his car with a megaphone. He didn't shout out the usual, "Move on, move on," this time. Instead he yelled out a name. "Brenda Stantonopolis we know you're here. Get out of your car and walk slowly toward us."

I saw Brenda's head slide down under the dashboard out of range of the windshield, but not before I spied my sister and she spied those glistening teeth. My sister had pulled up behind the squad cars on her bike and pointed out Sal's truck. The officer had to drag Brenda out of the truck with Sal trying to reason with him, behind her. We all watched as the cops put her in handcuffs and slid her into one of the squad cars. I will admit that I got absolute pleasure out of this riveting scene. Once they left, the other cop got on the megaphone and told us to move along now, move along. Cars started to pull out to the next destination, but I knew my night was over. I told Dolores I'd call her the next day and got out of her car. My sister was busy yelling at Sal and I heard the words, "slut" and "low-life" before I reached them. Sal was shrugging his shoulders assuring her that he had no idea what had gone down. My sister also had a lot of clout in this circle. Every guy wanted to do her, but my sister was tough and had only dated a few of the older guys before she moved on to a private high school outside the neighborhood. Sal poured her a beer and she sucked it down. She told me to get on the bike and I did. I remember hanging on to her t-shirt all the way home while she bitched at me. She was mad as hell and I couldn't blame her. I wasn't feeling so hot myself. The buzz was wearing off quickly and I was starting to feel sick. I knew when I got home it would be worse with my mother and it was. I swore up and down that I would never speak to Brenda again. I was grounded for the next two weekends for putting my mother and sister through something I hadn't known anything about, but I kept my mouth shut. It was a relief. I didn't feel like facing that group for a while.

Mr. Stantonopolis phoned the next day and then put Brenda on with my mother and after her, with me. She was the last person I expected to hear from.

"I wanted to apologize for putting you and your family through this ordeal," Brenda said in a shaky, unfamiliar voice. I could tell her dad had already beaten the hell out of her and I don't think she'd seen the end of it. I also heard in her voice that I would be dead-meat when I got back to school on Monday. Brenda would be after my scrawny ass.

I called a few of my friends on Sunday to feel out where their allegiance stood. Dolores, of course, was always on my side and called Brenda a skanky bitch. Jackie and Marsha feigned sympathy, but Brenda swayed them easily and there was no counting on support from them. The rest of the girls always went in the direction of the bigger mouth and I knew who won that prize, so basically I was screwed.

When Monday arrived I pleaded flu symptoms, but my mother just looked at me and said, "Get out of bed and face the music." That was it. My sister told me to get in Brenda's face and cause a massive scene. That was something my sister thrived on and I shrunk from.

I slowly walked to school and got through the first three classes without any repercussions. Brenda wasn't in any of my classes. Believe me, I was thankful for that. Lunchtime was another story. I knew I would have to run into her so I waited at Dolores's locker for moral support of some kind. We made the decision to move quickly through lunch with our eyes down and then go out and get stoned. I could manage violence from a distant, hazier perspective if it came my way. We got in line with our trays and I saw some of the girls already at a table whispering and conspiring. I nudged Dolores over to an empty table and looked briefly around the cafeteria. I didn't see Stantonopolis until she was almost upon us. She set her tray down on our table and pulled up the chair beside me. Dolores turned pale and put her head down quickly. Dolores's nickname was "Pole." She was taller than Brenda, ate faster and more food than I'd ever seen anyone eat, and never gained a pound. She had two pastimes–eating and getting high. I, on the other hand, had lost my appetite at this point and set my fork down. I looked over at Brenda. If she was going to hit me, let her do it now. She looked like hell. Her mouth was closed for once. I couldn't see any visible bruises, but knew they were there. She looked over at me. Her sunken eyes were swollen and pink. I actually wanted to apologize to her for what she'd been through, but stopped myself. What the hell did I have to be sorry for? She obviously didn't give a shit about my family or me. I tried to put on a sarcastic face with my teeth gritted and my brows furrowed. I stared back at her.

"You probably hate me," Brenda said. "I'm grounded for the rest of the semester if that's any help. My mom's actually picking me up and dropping me off everyday at school. And forget weekends. I'll be out of commission for a long, long time." Tears welled up in her eyes. "Can you believe that bullshit? And they're making me go to counseling twice a week for over a month after school. All for shitting in someone's yard." She looked up at us and a smile slowly materialized on her shaken face. I couldn't help myself. The visual that came up was totally entertaining. Dolores and I started to snicker.

"Can you imagine that family looking out their window, maybe even eating dinner, while I'm squatting on my haunches letting a big one loose on their lawn?" asked Brenda. Now Dolores was looking at us and we all started cracking up. There was no question that that must have been quite a scene. I watched a quieter Brenda start to regain her stride. Her mane of hair flew back when she laughed and those teeth spread out in all their splendor. I didn't hate her guts. I believe, at this point, I actually admired them. Anyone that could openly display the contents of their bowels to strangers was worthy of some kind of appreciation, weren't they?

HEIST WITH COMPENSATION

I had a distant relationship with money. I never had any and always seemed to be looking for it in the wrong places. My sister took a more proactive stance. As soon as she was old enough to say something that was actually listened to and considered by our parents she escaped our decrepit neighborhood and got promoted into a deluxe high school. It was a magnificent, whitewashed brick building packed with rich kids. Never mind that she had to get up every weekday morning while it was still dark, catch a bus by six a.m. and then ride it over fifty blocks to get there. She knew what she was doing. I went to the public high school a few blocks away from our house. It was a dingy, graffiti-ridden place full of the same dull faces that had stared back at me in grade school, but that didn't stop me from trying to hitch along on the tail of my sister's prowess. I was a fool some of the time, but when an opportunity of this magnitude presented itself, I made a special attempt to present myself.

My sister boasted that her school had the best drugs and the prodigal brood threw lavish parties every weekend. The easiest way to get at my sister was to deflate her ego.

"Drugs are drugs," I would say, "no matter how rich you are." Or, "Who cares how big someone's house is–just more room for more junk." This killed her.

"You should see so and so's mansion," she'd say. "It's fucking huge! And let me tell you there's no crap in that house. Our place is a dump compared to their's. You've never seen anything like it. And it would go on and on. Blah, blah, blah." She couldn't help herself with all the stories of the better stuff and the better drugs and the better guys, though it didn't take long to break her down. She told me I just had to come and see for myself.

I said, "Yeah, well maybe if I don't have anything better to do." She said, "You'll never have anything better to do." That was the way I propelled myself briefly into this strange, pretentious universe.

There was a party the following Saturday night and I was braced to go. My sister opened my bedroom door and said, "Well, if you're coming with me, I'm leaving in ten minutes, no more, no less," and then walked out of the room. I jumped off my bed and scrambled through the piles on the rug until I found a pair of jeans that looked fairly clean. I already had a fabulous peasant shirt I'd stolen from the India Shop that had been waiting for a party like this. I put on my desert boots and blasted into her room well within the allotted time limit. We smoked a joint on the way to the bus stop, which helped stop time from becoming an obstacle. It might have been a long trip by bus or maybe not. I was content to lay my head against the sleazy window and listen to the wet wheels spitting off rain, squeaky doors banking open and shut, and coins falling into the slot. My sister roused me when it was our stop. We walked past ancient looking lampposts with glowing balls on top. Shops had clothes that hung on hangers in neat, colorful, elitist rows. I shopped at Miltons on Morris Street. It was a neighborhood store where a garish, troll-lady with orange hair and fat red lips looked me up and down and then hobbled through an aisle of shelves with piles of white boxes until she found my size. She pulled out a long hook-like contraption that hung in each aisle and started rifling boxes at me. My mom had taken me to Miltons to buy my first bra. That also happened to be my first encounter with the shop lady troll. She flung open the single drape of my tiny dressing room that separated me from the world on Morris Street and said, "Oh, just look at them. Phyllis, come here. Aren't they adorable? They're like two pennies stuck to her bones. I don't think there's a bra that timid. What do you think, Phyllis?" and they both grabbed each other and started snickering. God, I hated shopping. I'm sure there were no trolls on this street.

My sister and I walked a few blocks past rows of two and three-story redbrick buildings with round upper rooms and castle-like roofs. I saw no trash on the street or rats that dared to scout this particular area. It seemed to be invitation only, no matter the species. My sister gave me a quick rundown on the guy who was holding the party before we got there. His family owned half of Chicago and the apartment was a three-story building that he and his brother shared exclusively. His name had a "Third" at the end of it. I got a good laugh out of that one.

When my sister and I finally arrived at their apartment a guy collecting invitations was standing at the door with his hair gelled up in some coif. He knew my sister and apparently liked her cause he was giving her the once over. I just walked right past him.

What a palace! It was like a huge warehouse with a spiral staircase that led all the way up to a high vaulted ceiling at the top like some kind of museum.

Paintings hung from every wall on every floor. I could pick out a few that looked familiar. My mother loved art magazines and they were always piled up in our bathroom. My parents had posters of Klee and Picasso hanging up in our house, but the paintings in this place were the real thing. I could tell by their frames.

A hundred kids or so were milling around the building. I made my way up the spiral staircase with my sister behind me yelling out to people and introducing me to some of them. The first floor seemed to be from another century. It had dark, Baroque looking portraits lined up along the walls. The second floor had abstracts and I believe I saw a Francis Bacon, who my mom loved, right up front. We kept moving up to the top floor. The music was different on each floor and so were the drugs according to my sister, who said the higher you went in the apartment, the higher you got. I lost my sister somewhere along the way, but found myself leaning into the deepest, most resonant, piece of furniture my head had ever laid on. A coffee table that looked to be the shape of something from biology class spread out in front of me and I'm sure it was designed by somebody that many somebodies knew. There was a group of kids around me doing lines of coke on the table and I joined in. I did a few lines while beers appeared in front of me one after another in rapid succession. This was a great party. I was feeling quite content until I looked up at the brick walls of this room and started to examine the paintings. There was a row of Lichtenstein paintings staring back. The longer I examined them the more I despised them. What kind of asshole painted demented red dots and blinding, euphoric comic book characters with bubbles hovering above their heads saying embarrassing things to each other? I don't know if it was the coke or the beastly wealth that was closing in around me that made me do what I did.

I'd read an article on the pompous ass in one of my mom's magazines when I had some time in the bathroom at home. There the so-called artist stood with those ridiculous fill-in-the-dots paintings lined up on either side of him in the photograph.

I did a few more lines of coke and the beers kept coming. I talked to some people and then made out with a guy who sat down next to me for a while. My sister was probably off with some somebody-the-third. I was happy with my plush couch and the strangers around me. I had no desire to lose my station. I'd probably be one of the last to leave so I soaked in whatever I could.

By three in the morning the group was dwindling. I had met the host of the party by this time. Reginald the Third looked nervously at me until I told him who I was. Thank God my sister was a beauty. Nobody wanted her to leave and so they never questioned me again once they knew

I was with her. When my obsession became a reality there were maybe ten or so people passed out on couches and I'm sure a few more in bedrooms around the place. I danced over to the wall of massive Lichtenstein's. They were even more obscene up close and personal. I touched one to see if an alarm would go off. Nothing came of it but the pounding of music beating in time with my heart. I lifted the one in front of me off the wall and looked around. No one was really conscious at this point. I took the stairs down as fast as I could, spiraling around getting dizzier and dizzier with this colossal painting in my hands. The downward spiral was definitely aiding in the onset of a burgeoning headache.

When I got to the first floor there was only one guy lying on the couch who looked at me briefly, but didn't seem to grasp what I was grasping. I stepped outside and then ran around the side of the building into the alley with this obscenely expensive, hell-ridden painting in my possession. I had just committed a felony. I looked up and down the well-lit alley. This was going to be one of the best stories I'd ever told come Monday morning at school, but how the hell was I going to make it to Monday with this dot-by-dot in my hands? I spotted a homeless guy making his way down the alley with a shopping cart full of crap. I ran, with loping sidesteps so I could see around the painting, up to him.

"Hey mister, don't you think you need a little art to hold up that collection of yours," I asked? I stared into his cart loaded with piles of empty cans, clothes and other debris with one naked Barbie doll minus the limbs layering the top like some kind of glorious, dumpster wedding cake.

"What you got there for your daddy, little peanut brittle," he asked? The stench coming off of him was not helping my precarious situation. I was getting dizzy and close to retching. This would have to be a quick transaction.

"How about I load up this canvas on your cart? You can buy lots of Barbie dolls and anything else your heart desires with this baby," I slurred.

"What the hell is it," he asked? He smiled. "It's a huge comic, isn't it? I've only got one of those in my collection and it's more like a book. Here, I'll show you." He started to rummage through his filthy pile while I loaded the abhorrent canvas onto his cart. It was huge, so I actually had to touch some of his nasty items to lodge it in there until it stuck at some point.

"Farewell, my friend. Make sure you get a good price for it. It may not look like much, but someone's going to want it. Stay away from the cops and never tell anyone where it came from," I said.

"Here now, little peanut brittle, I've got a gift for you," he said as he ransacked through his rank pile. He worked at it and then pulled out a half-eaten candy necklace still clinging to its elastic. "This is for you," he said proudly.

I stared at the heinous object that had been chomped on by some unknown person's gums and teeth and let him drape it in to my hand. "Well, mister," I said, "I believe I made out better than you on this one."

He frowned at me, giving the painting another once over to figure out how he'd been gypped.

I wound the candy necklace around my hand, waved goodbye and ran back to the party to see if I could pry my sister off of one of the somebody-the-Third's and get the hell out of there before I found handcuffs instead of second-hand candy wrapped around my wrists.

THIRTEEN

I sat outside in my car and waited for what, I didn't know. I stared at a battered, Victorian house with a long porch and nobody on it. I was possessed -persecuted by my own brain. I had bypassed that "seeing red" kind of anger to a denser, blacker void. I had a gun in my lap. It wasn't loaded, the guy wouldn't give me any bullets, and I didn't know how to shoot the damn thing anyway, but I liked the cold, hard feel of it in my lap.

My friend, Adel, had been gang-raped in this house a week before. I knew no one who lived in the house, but I had a clear vision of cattle-necked frat-boys lined up and castrated by a dull, sweeping machete. I also enjoyed the image of shooting their balls off, one by one. Thirteen was the number Adel rasped the morning she limped into our off-campus house with one shoe on, no underwear and no purse.

A whole group of us had gone out the night that Adel got raped. We went to some of the usual bars and got saturated -just another weekend night on a college campus. Adel was visiting. She was no longer one of our roommates. She got kicked out of a school that was pretty hard to get kicked out of, because she'd stopped going to classes. My other roommates and I would come back to our house after lectures and tests and find Adel with an apron on, vacuuming, dusting, making our beds and cooking for us, like some underage housewife. It was creepy. We were a slovenly group in a beaten-up, nasty, old house, and obviously didn't care what state the place was in. We threw chronic parties after the bars had closed and never cared who showed up or if we even knew them at all. One of my roommates woke up on the floor next to a dust-ridden corner she'd never seen before, where her bed used to be. Some guy had actually stolen her mattress out from under her, while she remained passed out. We found out only because the guy had stepped on a few bodies on his way out of the house. No one had stopped him. Just vaguely remembered a mattress moving above their heads and a boot stepping on some body part before they passed out again.

We weren't a scholarly group and Adel had started to lose her grip long before she got kicked out. We didn't say much when she lay in bed crying for the first few weeks of our sophomore year. We were all hanging on to our sanity as best we could, so we consoled her, sat with her and generally felt some deranged comfort realizing that she might be worse off than the rest of us.

But then it just got plain weird. That's when everyone started talking behind her back–things like, "she's lost it," or "somebody get her the hell out of here, I can't take her shit anymore," kind of comments. When she donned the apron, sweeping off the porch and waving to us as we came up the street from campus, it got really disturbing. We'd walk into a Pine-soled house with a clear path to the kitchen and the smell of something edible cooking in an oven that had, prior to this, only been used to hide our stash of pot or cocaine -it felt like walking into some fifties time warp. That's when we knew the Adel we had partied with before was not coming back, and this Stepford wife had stepped in to take her place. Tears welled up in her eyes no matter what was said to her.

One of my roommates and I had decided to sit her down and tell her it was best if she went back home. It hadn't been easy. She'd been using the money her mom sent to buy groceries and we were starting to enjoy eating again. The anal-retentive-housewife bit was scary though, and some of our friends had been dropping by just to mess with Adel's head. It wasn't good, so we told Adel in a calm voice that it was probably time to get home to her family and figure out something else to do with her life. She had cried and hugged us, but we managed to get her packed and on a train back home within two weeks.

And now Adel was here again. A year had passed since we'd sent her home and she seemed much better. Her sister told me that Adel had been locked up for three months in a psychiatric ward. She'd done some intensive counseling and a psychiatrist had put her on a hefty dose of anti-anxiety pills that kept her less soporific and more defined. She was only visiting for a weekend, so we were all happy to see her hanging out in our dirty house without trying to clean it. We'd had a pre-party that infamous night and then gone out to some bars and somewhere along the way I'd lost track of Adel. I figured she'd hooked up with some guy and was off at another party having a good old time like the rest of us.

It was about six in the morning when one of my roommates stumbled home from wherever she'd been and woke me up to tell me Adel wasn't back. I had a really bad feeling, on top of the hellish hang-over that was setting in, and I couldn't get back to sleep. Guilt and a combination of those last three shots of tequila I did before the bars closed were ravaging my stomach and my head.

I had known Adel since we were kids and always felt compelled to watch out for her, even though I wasn't even capable of taking care of myself. We'd smoked our first cigarette together, stole our first ice cream bar, and drank our first beer out of her mom's stash. Her mom was usually drunk, so it was easy to steal her cigarettes and beer. Adel had always been fragile. She threw herself in front of a truck once when we were around thirteen because a new girl from school and I had gone to basketball practice without her. She had told her mom she was jealous and that's why she did it - actually threw herself in front of an oncoming truck. It took us a while to be friends again. I didn't know what to say to Adel. We both felt strange about the whole thing. Adel didn't have a dad to speak of. He'd been in and out of mental hospitals and wasn't allowed near their house. I never got the whole story on him, but I don't even know if she knew much of it herself. We didn't talk about her dad or mine for that matter. We spent most of our time drunk and high and tried to keep our own private hells to ourselves.

But now, here it was, six a.m. and no Adel. I listened for a car to pull up or the door downstairs to open until around eight and when she didn't appear, I dragged myself out of bed and down to the kitchen. I managed to make a pot of coffee and sat shaking with my mug by the window. The shakiness was the usual consequence of a bitter hangover, but, of course, included the fears I had for my friend. I stared out at a barren street with no people in sight. It was Sunday morning in a college town, and no one was up this early. I hadn't seen this hour of the day on a weekend since I got here three years before. I was a junior now, somehow still getting through classes and getting fairly good grades. Whatever brain cells were left, were sticking it out with me through these years, and I was thankful for them. I listened to the leaves and empty cans rustle and rattle around in the street. The winds were gusting on another gray, October day. At some point, I saw a figure in the distance moving slowly in my direction. I didn't run out to meet her. I squatted on the couch, watching her, trying to get a feel for what kind of condition she was in. She was limping down the street with one shoe on. The wind was blowing her clothes all over the place. She was trying to hold her skirt down and her blouse was sliding off one shoulder. Her hair appeared to be greased against her skull. Her face was red and puffy. I felt an animalistic fear when I got a look at her eyes. They had that faraway Sylvia Plath look to them -unreachable and not of this planet. Something bad had happened to Adel. Her fractured being had always been transparent, but now it was a shattered window of glass. I opened the door and she dropped into my arms. She was crying, but it was slow, steady tears that streamed down her face. She was not hysterical. She reeked of stale beer and sex. I sat her down on the couch and ransacked the cupboards until I found a box of chamomile tea. I made a mug of tea and poured some vodka in it. I had to hold it to her lips while she sipped. The two of us were trembling, so I held the mug with both hands.

Now, everyone else was waking up and starting to layer the room with their bodies. They gave Adel a frenzied once-over look and then studied me with a questioning stare. I gave them a narrow-eyed-you-know-what-I'm-saying look until they cleared the room so I could talk to her alone. Her voice was husky. I had to lean in close to decipher whatever it was she said. Her eyes were a tragedy. They looked into a place I didn't ever want to go. I held her jittery hand in mine. We vibrated together. I tried to piece together whatever parts of the night she was able to get to. She'd gone off with some guy from the bar. She couldn't remember his name. They'd been messing around outside, and then for a while in his car. He took her back to his house. There was a party going on when they got there. She didn't recognize anyone, except Diane. She remembered seeing Diane. We knew Diane through a friend of a friend, and she'd show up at our parties pretty often, so I figured I could find her somehow.

Then Adel said, "Thirteen."

"What?" I asked.

"Thirteen." She attempted a laugh that came out raspy and demonic. "Always a bad number, right?" Adel asked. Her low, scratchy voice became disembodied from her face as it flashed through a night that hell couldn't come close to. She had no purse, and that meant no pills. I kept draining vodka into her tea until she passed out. I got some of the girls to help put her to bed in my room and one of us sat up watching her all night, but she slept straight through until late in the morning.

The next day Adel was not much better. She was a fragment of herself. She didn't blink much -just stared into space.

"No cops," she said. She was definitely in no state to deal with cops and neither were we. There were drugs in the house and everyone was drinking again, just to get through it. None of us went to class on Monday. Everyone knew the story by then and they all had something to say. Rage was just another person in the room. We were capable of anything. The more we drank the more raucous we became.

"I'll fucking cut off their balls," said one.

"Slowly," said another. "Make them feel every excruciating little slice," she continued.

"We need to scare the shit out of them. Get a gun," said another. That made perfect sense to me. They continued their castrating fantasies while I went into the other room. I got on the phone with this guy who could get us anything and usually did.

"Are you insane?" he asked. "What the hell am I saying? Of course you're insane. And drunk as usual," he added. "What the hell are you going to do with a gun?" He was laughing now. It was true. I didn't have the first idea what I'd do with a gun, but I knew I wanted one.

"How about some grade-A ass-kicking pot? Take a few hits off of this stuff and you'll forget you ever wanted to shoot anything," he said.

He hung up on me a few times. I finally let up and stopped calling. He showed up a few hours later and sat down next to me on the couch. I could pretty much get him to do anything. He took one look at Adel, red-eyed and placid, and took me into the kitchen.

It wasn't loaded and he refused to give me any bullets, but he did show me how to scare someone. He asked if he could help. I said no. I got some of that pot he was talking about while he was going on and on. I didn't show the gun to anyone. My roommates thought he had only brought pot and they were happy to help me smoke it. I went upstairs, at some point, and hid the gun in the bottom drawer of my dresser under some ratty t-shirts. It felt cold, heavy and powerful. It felt like justice.

The next morning I dragged Adel out of bed, got her dressed, and put her in one of my roommate's cars. I kept her drunk hoping she wouldn't panic. I wanted to find the house. I had a call in to Diane, but hadn't heard from her yet. Adel and I roamed around the campus. It was a small town, but it was still a town, with a lot of damn houses that looked about the same. She described it as a two-storied, dingy house with lots of windows, full of people on a long porch. That pretty much described almost every house in this slumlord town at night. I was starting to lose steam. We'd been up and down street after street and nothing was pulling her out of her haze. I went on with the questioning, like some bad TV detective, and she drank her beer and stared out the smudged windshield saying almost nothing. We were on our way back to my house, when she looked at me and said, "The house had a name." Strange as it may sound some of these broken-down houses had names. Of course, there were the frat and sorority houses with their plaques outside whining, "Delta, Delta, Delta", or "Sigma Gamma Phi" or some other Greek name that nobody understood. But even our sad, demented house had a name. We had a green sign with white letters, hanging from chains across the threshold, which read, "Rover Rest Home". We lived on Rover Street.

Adel had looked back that morning at the house she was leaving with no purse, no underwear, and one shoe and stared up at a sign. She remembered the sound of it jangling on its chain. She actually came up with the name, as though she were reading it in front of us at that very moment. "Anheiser Astor" is what Adel said. I knew where Astor Street was, so we drove over there. It was a side street that led to a dead-end, so it wasn't hard to locate the house. "Anheiser Astor" was up there, still creaking on its hinges in the wind. No one was out on the porch or anywhere to be seen. The front door was wide open, but everyone left his or her front door open off-campus. No one had much to steal, unless you were in need of a mattress. We sat there for a while. Nothing happened, except that I realized Adel was getting agitated, which meant blinking again and fidgeting in her seat. I took her back to Rover Rest Home and put her to bed. A few of my roommates and I sent her home on the train the next day. I called Adel's sister and told her that Adel was in bad shape. I didn't tell her why. I didn't think it was my place to tell her anything, except that Adel had drank too much and lost her purse and her pills, and needed a new prescription and maybe some more counseling. Her sister accepted it all and said she'd meet her at the train. Now I was on my own.

My roommates wanted to know what I had found out, and they badgered me for a few days, but I said we should just leave it alone and try to forget it ever happened. I told them Adel couldn't remember anybody or the place she'd been that night. Adel and I had driven around, but never found the house. Diane did show up finally and told us a harrowing tale of Adel on a rampage. She said everyone already knew Adel was whacked and a whore, so they just did what guys will do. They took her on, one by one. Diane actually watched a few of them go into a room and close the door; knowing Adel was in there alone.

I asked Diane a question. "Did these guys live in the house, or were they just partying there?"

"Oh yeah, they were the guys from the house -most of them. It's not like I sat around watching the whole damn thing. Really, I had other things to do," she laughed.

I took aim and threw my full can of beer at Diane as hard as I could, hitting her on the side of her face. She wailed out, jumped off the couch and lunged at me. I shoved my boot into her stomach and slammed her away from me with all of my force. She flew back into a lamp, knocking it over.

"You fucking cunt," I screamed, "get the fuck out of here, before I take a whole twelve-pack and smack it over your head." Diane did get up, with blood trailing down the side of her face, but not without threatening me. I had the other roommates with me. A few of them got up. They punched her, pushed her towards the door, swore at her and then one of them slammed the door behind her and locked it. Anger raged up in everyone again, but I knew it would calm down with just a little more time. Life in "Rover Rest Home" forgot most everything that happened to it after a few days, so the topic moved away from Adel and on to more pressing matters, like who had cash for beer and where was the next party.

I didn't forget. I would come home from class some days, and pull the gun out of my drawer. I'd drive over to "Anheiser Astor" and sit across the street and wait. I had a nice, huge weeping willow to park under, so I was pretty well hidden. It was an all-guy's house -lots of them. I didn't recognize them, but sat and watched as they drank beer on the porch. They were loud and full of themselves and anything but unusual. I sat with my gun in my lap in a stupor. The fantasies of what I would do were always satisfying. I had the power to become invisible. I'd stamp up on their porch and knock beers in their faces, smack their slacken mouths or whisper horrible shit I would do to them in their ears. I would scare them like they'd never been scared before. I'd already blown through all the visions of blasting bullets through their heads or crotches, or both. I'd already charged the porch with a machete and sliced them up one by one many times over in my head. It was all quite enjoyable, but got me nowhere. I just sat there.

I talked with Adel a few times over the Christmas holidays at home. She had slit her wrists the wrong way, and was locked up in a psych ward at a hospital near by. I didn't go to visit. She didn't ask me to come either. It seemed we both wanted it best left forgotten. When I got back to school I let it all go by like a balloon that slowly loses its helium. I gave the gun back at some point. I went back to classes during the day and bars at night. I sometimes had nightmares with Adel in them. All these jeering, hideous men hovering over me with their mocking faces, covering me with grimy, hairy hands and I'd wake up sticky and shivering, unable to go back to sleep. Waiting for daylight didn't help.

It wasn't until the spring that it all came back to me. I was sitting at one of the many bars in town with a few of my friends, doing shots and having a few beers when I saw one of the Thirteen actually walk past me. Those faces from "Anheiser Astor" were forever seared into my memory. He was tall and one of the few with a neck, with a saunter that said more than it should have. I started to feel all hot inside. My head was buzzing and I felt rage surging through me. I ordered another shot, this time a whisky, and got up to find him. I staggered over to where he sat on the other side of the bar. He was alone. He looked at me and smiled. I smiled back and sat down next to him. There was definitely something I could do.

HOLIDAY INN IN THE HOLIDOME

I get dumped out of a car in front of the Holiday Inn in the Holidome. My head wants to roll off its neck like a bowling ball into a gutter. If I could just suck down one beer in front of this garish hotel I might be able to cheerfully make it through. My boyfriend, Dennis, finds this all amusing and pretty much shoves me out of the car. He spends Sundays looking through the want ads circling potentially humiliating jobs for me. Fuck him! He's got a drawer full of cash in his dresser. Dennis manages a few of the major bars on Rush Street in Chicago, while my friends and I drink for free. He thinks I need to get up everyday and get dressed. "Have a good time, Michelle. I'll pick you up in a half hour," he says with a smirk, and speeds off. I'm left outside in the wind.

I walk into a huge atrium with an old, gray piano player, large, fake plants and a migraine-fested palette of hot pink and turquoise pulsing from the walls, tablecloths and streaks of circus-sun hoofing it in from the skylight above. Stabs and pokes of memories of last night snicker at me with remnants of upside-down watermelon shots, the decayed molars of a coked-up corpulent hyena-guy, vagrant conversations with vagrants about nothing and wrists tied to the bedpost.

I attempt to walk a steady line toward the yawning, endless counter with businessmen in suits checking in and out. I look down to see what Dennis has dressed me in. It's all black and looks washed and ironed. Dennis likes to iron, in his underwear, in front of the TV while he screams at football players. This image is usually a fond one. Today I hate him.

A lady, about eighty, with a hairball coughed up on her head, sits me down at a table in the employees' lounge with papers to fill out. The lines on the paper are arrogant. They are smugly assured that my life will parade itself out with panties around my ankles and showcase me as a wrist-flicking puncher of time-clocks. Hairball lady whispers to Blue eye shadow lady that I have a college degree. They both nod and think this means something.

Dennis is ecstatic when the phone rings and they tell me I've got the job. He picks me up and swings me around. He takes me to breakfast and loudly orders a huge entrée. When the food arrives he lines his five beverages up side by side, OCD style–coffee, chocolate milk, orange juice, lemonade and apple juice. He chugs a few with a chaser of four ibuprofen. His barreling voice bombards deep into the ears of the waitresses, patrons and me. He gulps his drinks with his pinky up and lives with some kind of mayoral hard-on in his head. He gorges his plate of huevos rancheros. I study the mound of beans, eggs and green slop that he shovels in and suddenly see the inside of his intestines. I am sick now and can only drink coffee. I remember that I stole a hundred dollar bill from his drawer this morning while he was in the shower. I am starting to feel better about things.

Blue eye shadow lady measures me for my Holiday Inn costume. "How lucky," the woman says. They had an employee who wore the exact same size. The woman goes

99

in the back somewhere and comes out with two rumpled turquoise skirts with matching vests and two evil blouses. The blouses are neon stripes of flamingo pink and turquoise with fat bow ties attached to the shirts. Darts slash out on either side of the boob area. This particular fabric does not seem to wrinkle even when balled up. "Panty hose are mandatory," she says. "A little tip for you, young lady." Blue eye shadow winks. "Wear comfortable shoes. You're going to be on your feet all day." I look down at Blue eye shadow's shoes. She is stacked in black stiletto heels at least four inches high. She clicks away from me and says, "See you Monday, Michelle. 6:45 AM, prompt."

I work the seven to three shift at the Holiday Inn, Monday through Friday. I am set up at the front desk. I am forced to look over Hairball's shoulder for a week to attempt to learn the trade. As soon as I arrive each day a line of cheap suits are waiting to check out. They smack their lips and look me up and down in my polyester train wreck and say "mmm, mmm, now isn't she cute? Are you new on the job, pretty thing?" they ask. I huddle next to Hairball squinting and punching in codes and swearing to myself. I look up at a bald one and say, "oh no, can't you tell? I'm a regular, old veteran at this," as Hairball tsk, tsks me, and has to void out yet another mis-punch on the cash register.

Heidi is the reservationist. She has worked in the Holidome for three years. She has her own office. She is chubby and sarcastic and hates this place as much as me. We become fast friends. She keeps a bottle of vodka locked up in her bottom desk drawer so Mrs. Feldenheim will never find it. Mrs. Feldenheim is a Nazi. She is the general manager of the hotel. She is about 6'2 and skeleton ugly with a long rod up her ass.

Heidi and I sit next to each other at the weekly meetings. About twelve employees are sitting in a conference room that sports the same antagonizing motif. I have gone through countless Advils just to make it through. Heidi and I have already snuck a few drinks before the meeting. Mrs. Feldenheim is pacing back and forth as she talks. She is proud of the Holidome. She thinks this is a career. She tells everyone how lucky he or she is to have these important positions. It is a tough job market out there and if everyone works with his nose to the grindstone (she actually says this) then everyone will be set for life. Heidi kicks me under the table. I start snickering. "You think this is funny, little smart mouth," Mrs. Feldenheim asks me. I wait for her to continue and then punch Heidi back and sit more erect in my chair with my hands folded, pretending to listen.

"You people need to take this seriously. I am now in the position I have always wanted to be in."

Heidi whispers in my ear, "Yeah, like straddling that pasty, old piano man, gyrating her bony ass all over his lap with a whip in her hand, while he continues playing one of his elevator-music-just-shoot-me-in-the-head lounge acts. You KNOW Feldenheim's a psycho-dominatrix."

Mrs. Feldenheim continues. "I now have THIS many applications," (she flings her arms out wide) "for THIS many jobs." (She pinches her fingers together). Heidi raises her hand. "Mrs Feldenheim? I have seen most of the applicants. How many of them actually speak English?" Mrs. Feldenheim glares at Heidi as she kicks me again.

Dennis is pushing me to quit the job. It wasn't his intention for me to enjoy it when he first shoved me out of the car at the Holidome. He assumed I'd drop it like I did the rest of the crappy jobs I'd had after a week or so. I was now going on three months without missing a day. It was approaching Christmas and everyone wanted time off except for Heidi, who was Jewish and needed the cash, and myself. I always hated the holidays anyway and I'd get paid double-time for working Christmas day. Dennis has a huge family and he loves the holidays, being the politician-in-his-pants kind of guy. He wants me all sparkly and by his side. I like pissing Dennis off. His job-hunting prank blew up in his face. Maybe when I finally quit this job, because it is only a matter of time, he will stop selling me out and let me pillage his dresser drawer, the penny-pinching ass, and live the life I was destined for. The nightlife.

Christmas day arrives. I check out ten suits at the counter. These are the really cheap ones that can't afford to take off the holidays, or they're having affairs and don't want to go home. The good part is that five out of ten of them give me a bottle of wine as a present. They feel sorry for me and I play it up. I shouldn't have to work on Christmas day. A few make passes at me and try to hustle me into meeting them for dinner or at another hotel. I am getting good at playing with their brainless heads.

Heidi is sitting up front with me today. She runs in the back whenever we need to open another bottle of wine. We go through at least three bottles before we stop answering the phone, "Holiday Inn in the Holidome, can I help you?" I'm the first one to change it.

The phone rings. We are sitting up front laughing and telling stupid jokes. I pick it up. "Happy Holidays, Heidi and Michelle's Hollow-Ass Holidome, can I help you?" Heidi is totally cracking up. The person hangs up. That happens a few times.

There are a few people milling around. One fat guy keeps flirting with Heidi and me up at the counter. He thinks we're actually going to take him on in a threesome. Of course, we lead him on for a while, because what else is there to do?

The phone rings again. I am slurring by now. "Heidi and Michelle's Hollow-Assface Holidome, can I help you?" There is silence.

Then the booming voice of Mrs. Feldenheim sprays out of the receiver. "What the hell did you say?"

Now, I am speechless. I look over at Heidi, smile, and say, "It's for you."

Heidi starts singing some Hanukkah song into the phone and stops mid-line. "Shit," she mouths to me. Her face turns a beautiful, ghastly white. I fall on the carpet and start rolling around laughing. This is too rich. My career at the

Holidome has almost ended. Though, certainly not before Heidi and me book a flight to Mexico on Heidi's excellent discount plan with some of the cash I've been stocking away from my boyfriend's dresser drawer.

THE BOTTOM LINE

Bernice Mendelsohn looked right through me. Eye contact between us was an unsanctioned landscape. She had to pass me at least a few times each day, but saw nothing where I stood or sat. I banked my working life on this law of matter. I wanted only to silently exist, do my appointed jobs, and get out before anyone noticed.

I was everything Bernice loathed–lanky, rumpled, and a shiksa, not to mention a peon buried beneath the writhing layers of corporate advertising. I was an assistant to a media buyer in a large advertising agency, H. R. Bingaman. I was that coffee mug never dredged out of the back of the cabinet, branded with a permanent, brown stain, that shouted out from the sides of it's non-descript beige ceramic: KRUT: Fastest growing market in Christian Bog, Kansas? No one knew how long the mug had been there or if the town existed, but nobody was invested enough to throw it out.

Bernice was the head buyer of the department and utilized all of the clout a media buyer could possibly squander to raise the corpse of fear in every sales rep that entered her office. They strutted in chronically hopeful, full of lavish compliments for Bernice, but rarely lasted more than ten minutes. They staggered out with faces that revealed either a vast drop in blood pressure or an alarming rise, depending on the person.

Bernice and I were destined to intertwine, if for no other reason than two opposites this absurd could only be transformed completely or swallowed whole by one another. I was not yet privy to this fact of life, and was living a banal, peaceful existence about a mile from the treacherous building that housed our agency. It was offensively tall and cast a shadow over any beam of sun that tried to wrestle through its armored frame. It was famous for all of its successful suicides that kept tourists looking up with interest. They ate their lunches out in the park across the street in case of a sighting. It was 99 floors high with a security guard posted up there to ward off any more would be suicides from breaking through the concrete-like glass. The last guy to succeed had strapped an axe to his leg to get past security. That axe of his was powerful enough to shatter the false impenetrability of corporate America. His was a sighting that was recorded on camcorders far, far below. Because of the design of this monstrosity of a building, his body kept bouncing off the windows on the way down, leaving every company with a window view every four floors or so–a great story to tell that lasted at least a month. We had a direct connection to this last fortunate or unfortunate man's demise. An untimely client of H.R. Bingaman had been on his way into the building when he was splattered with unknown body parts. This left him out of commission, literally, for over three weeks.

I walked to work everyday, which allowed me a longer period in bed each morning, and a little exercise for free when I finally got up and out. I had a roommate I got along with. She was in law school and we met up each night to tell horror stories of our day and smoke cigarettes we left in a little box on the coffee table. It was my favorite time of day coming home for smokes and a beer and a chance to recover from the dregs of the coffee mug I lived in 9 to 5, Monday though Friday, rather than smoke cigarettes with the other assistants during their five minute breaks. It was safer if I had someone to commiserate with outside the agency. Almost anyone at H. R. Bingaman would take you down, given the chance.

I frequented a bar called the Panda Lounge on the weekends and some weeknights when I needed an escape. It was a tiny, smoky room with a black and white motif and an owner that gave me a microphone whenever I'd had enough drinks to perform.

I was Bill Murray in my mind. I told bad jokes and sang songs from a past nobody wanted to remember–the 70's. "Raindrops Keep Falling on My Head" was one of my favorites and "Close To You" one of the two greatest hits by the anorexic Carpenters. I liked to sing that song to young, happy couples huddled in dark corners who sneered at me and slouched in their panda painted chairs, hoping for their own invisibility.

And just when my existence set itself into a black and white pattern that calmed and distracted me, life soon inevitably betrayed me. On Monday I walked my usual path to work. I took the long elevator ride up to the office and stumbled to my desk. I started to go through the pile of filing and miscellaneous tasks that always settled themselves before me each morning. But something was different today. When I looked over at the buyer I worked for, Shelly, she looked excessively happy and it was a Monday. Nobody was happy on Monday unless an unwanted relative died or someone had gotten lucky over the weekend. I watched as the other media buyers came out of their offices smiling and hugging her. Was it her birthday? What the hell had I missed? I figured someone would let me in on the news sooner or later. Shelly stood in front of my desk a few minutes later with a grin on her face. Stupidly, I grinned back in anticipation of something pleasurable and new.

Shelly's speech began with her need to move on to deeper waters and explore new avenues. The tether of her existence here at H. R. Bingaman had choked itself and finally reached its demise. She ran through a lengthy exposition on how she would miss me tremendously for all the dedicated and efficient work I had contributed to our team. She wished that she could take me with her, but that was not possible. I tried to think of the other buyers and wondered whom I would be working for next. My favorite was the faded, old Irish lady with dyed orange hair, who had saddled herself for so many years at H. R. Bingaman that she kept a bottle of scotch in her bottom drawer. Her face reddened as the day progressed, until she was completely soused and purple by day's end. I enjoyed the stories she told of her life in the lowlands before she was forced to bleed for the cash. I wouldn't mind working for her. The rest were not as interesting, but bearable, I'm sure. Shelly continued on for a while longer with that word "commitment" sauntering in quite often till it's all I heard. Then she pulled out a wrapped, square box the size of a skull and set it in front of me.

"I will miss you, you know. But we will definitely stay in touch and I'll still be in the advertising field. I hope our paths will continue to cross. You, too, have a long road ahead of you." She didn't have to remind me of that. She rambled on a bit more about the next upward step for both of us in life's continuing education and that there were plenty of opportunities that just couldn't be passed up. Everything she said came out like the spiel of a politician campaigning for her next election.

Her smile broadened. "But, of course, I'm not the only one moving up the ranks. Your work and dedication to this agency have not gone unnoticed in this office." And I thought I'd been invisible this entire time.

"We take care of our good ones. You will be forging ahead as well." Was there an axe in that box?

"It seems all the typing and filing and corrected errors on memos and extra hours you've put in have been noted by your superiors." She smiled again. I stared at her and waited for the exciting pronouncement to come.

"You, of all the assistants in this office, have been chosen by Bernice Mendelsohn to be hers!"

I stared at her in horror. Nothing came out of my mouth. My soon-to-disappear, easy-going boss, who never did much work, was sending me to the gallows with a smile on her face. She laughed.

"This is a huge promotion for you and believe me, you won't be sorry. She's always good to the people who work for her. She'll treat you like a queen. You'll be heavily rewarded for entering her sanctum."

I held the box in my hands and looked past her out the window. No one was falling at the moment. She listed all the promising and exciting bonuses that this promotion would bring. I felt like I was signing up for some sort of time-share in Hawaii. I thought I might get drunk after work. I thought of quitting. Life had been simple and methodical. It had arranged itself so naturally that there was no longer thought involved in any of it. I could space out from 9 to 5 and still be considered a treasure. So it had come to this. Complacency had brought malignancy. I stared back into my boss's face as she bubbled on and I knew that there was no going back. I either quit that moment or agreed to forever blacken my soul with a day-to-day existence of heart palpitations and tremors.

I sat down at my desk with the box in front of me. The assistant to my right looked over at me with deep sympathy. I'm sure the news had made waves around the office. Everyone who looked at me had that same tilt of the head, fake smile and complete knowledge that I was not long for H.R. Bingaman.

I was expected to go back to work as though nothing had passed. The waiting began. How long before I was called into Bernice's office? I sat at my desk and pretended to work on projects that no longer existed for me.

My neighbor asked what was in the box. "I don't know. A gift from the boss," I answered.

She stared at me with raised eyebrows. "Well, aren't you going to open it?"

"No." I put it under my desk and began to collate and staple piles. I could wait for a very, very long time.

*　*　*　*

I remember my first encounter with Bernice. She was part of the interview process before I joined the firm. In order to work in the department I had to pass her scrutiny after my boss had given the okay. I walked in and sat down across from her. She was plastering lipstick over her bulging lips. Her face held together big features on a small body. Her clothes blazed with colors and patterns that she had tucked in to latex beneath and lots and lots of jewelry. She had one fake gold and gem earring on an ear and one that was lying on her desk. They were clip-ons, I could see, and she must have taken one off to talk on the phone. Everything on her shimmered, though her eyes were what captivated me. They were lined above and below in black, and spoke litanies of backroom tortures and executions. She smiled at me when she finally looked up from her pocket mirror with the look one gives a cockroach before squashing it. I sat in her office and handed over my dubious resume and tried to look calm. She was the animal who smells fear before she attacks. She put her earring back on her ear. I looked beyond her at the photos on the wall of her and various minor celebrities and reminded myself that life would go on without this job. She looked up with a coral, lipsticked smile after glancing over the embarrassing sheet of paper.

"So, you have no experience. You're barely out of a crappy state college and your past and only prior job was as a clerk at a Holiday Inn?" Out loud it sounded much worse than on paper. I should have lied.

"Yes." I tried not to appear weak.

"So exactly what is it, Michelle, that you think you can offer us here at H.R. Bingaman that we haven't tossed out a thousand times before?" She looked me over for any tics, sweating or nail biting. I was picking at my cuticles under the desk. I had no idea what would come out of my mouth.

"I live only eight or so blocks from here and I would never be late. I have no problem working late hours and I am trainable." I made myself look directly into the clump of eyelashes that clung together above her eyes.

"Is there anything else you'd like to add to that?" she asked. "There must be something more?"

I sat and thought. "I'll never be late," I reminded her.

Her phone rang and she dismissed me with the wave of red-tipped nails as she pulled off her earring again. Well, at least that was over. I left the office and took the elevator down with a freedom that can only come from the assurance that you will never see that person again. But then, freedom is only a concept that pretends to reach a hand out and brush us off from time to time in moments after waking from some horrible dream or after humiliating experiences when we are given a chance to escape.

I left the building and proceeded home having done my duty for the day. I lay on the couch, read a book and smoked a few cigarettes. I was entitled to some recompense for sweating unnoticed.

Unfortunately, they called me back for another round of interviews, so I was back in that office the following week in panty hose, perspiring again, but armed with the knowledge that this was one desperate organization if they were dragging me back. I had to meet with a few other buyers who asked me inane questions such as where did I see myself in five years? Well, definitely not here, if I was lucky. Then I got the questions about my weaknesses. I thought it best to leave out my panic attacks and hatred of humanity for the time being and come up with some placid responses that might get me the job.

"I see myself working long hours dedicated to helping the agency in anyway possible. I want to learn as much as I can and I am always punctual and rarely get sick. The only weakness I can come up with is my lack of experience, but working with you, under your wing, I know that I will soon become accomplished and knowledgeable. I am excited to get started." I almost puked from these wretched lies. I slumped back in the chair and tried not to hyperventilate. The various buyers I met smiled at me and wrote little notes on my resume. They appeared satisfied with my deplorable responses. I didn't know how much longer the process took. My cheekbones ached from the perpetual happiness that strained across my face.

*   *   *   *

"Well, open the damn box," my roommate demanded. We sat smoking cigarettes and drinking Budweisers, staring at the square centerpiece on the coffee table in front of us.

I picked it up. It was heavy. I tore open the wrapping and the box and we stared at the object.

"People are absolutely wacked," said my roommate snorting. "What the hell is that supposed to signify?"

It was the most demented gift I'd ever received, by far. My roommate and I stared at a ceramic jack-o-lantern with the price tag still dangling from its orange, little cap with the green stem on top. I looked at the price. It was certainly no cheap ceramic pumpkin. After all, it was pulled out of a Marshall Field's box.

"Why," I responded, "don't you see how remarkable it is? It's a breathtaking specimen." I stroked it in my hands. "This used to be H.R. Bingaman—our dead and buried commander-in-chief. Instead of stuffing him entirely, which would be the usual protocol, they were much more imaginative in those days. They decapitated him and had his head glazed and baked and sent out a multitude of facsimiles across the US of A to be sold in tacky collectible shops and even large department stores like Marshall Fields. These beautiful, orange heads sit and glow in windows across the map. It's all quite touching if you think about it. He was a very important man, you know. They couldn't just let him rot like the rest of us, under the ground. Did you know you can crank out one of Lincoln's heads made out of blue wax from a machine in Springfield, Illinois?" I took another swig from my bottle.

"Maybe we should drop him from the 99th floor on Halloween night?"

"That's a beautiful image. In honor of his legendary prowess as a hands on man. I heard he fondled every orange head of hair he could scrape his fingers through in that office of his at the top. My God, I wonder if he wreaked havoc on my Irish friend at work? She's old enough and orange enough. The bottle of scotch in her bottom drawer must keep the demon of his memory at bay and help the trauma of flashbacks recede into one big blur of a past." I swilled back more beer and continued. I was enjoying this conversation. "Did you know they didn't have to extract his brain? He never had one–immaculate rejection by birth. No brain ever stood in the way of his duties as head of our multinational firm."

"What about the mouth?" asked my roommate. "Certainly lacks any dental attention."

I took a drag off my cigarette and studied him. "That hollow smile has become a legacy at H. R. Bingaman. Every

interview I've been on, I've seen the same dark space within—
an orifice without the tunnel beyond. There's no way out."

I set the ceramic jack-o-lantern back on the table.

"And do you know what all this means?" I got up
from the couch. "It means I desperately need another beer.
How about you?" I asked as I headed to the kitchen. By the
end of the night, H.R. Bingaman's pumpkin head had
become a large, orange ashtray piling up with butts and
embers.

*   *   *   *

A week later I was sitting outside Bernice's office at
my new desk putting my things away. She hadn't appeared
yet.

"She's never on time, get used to it," said one buyer
who passed by.

"Always look busy, never look her in the eye," said
another, patting me on the back.

"You're welcome to my scotch any time of day, little
lass, but if I were you I'd get me own stash as soon you can
get away. You're going to need it." My orange headed Irish
pal bobbled back toward her desk down the hall.

Bernice's office was the first one to the right of the
bank of elevators so that she could keep an eye on anyone
who came through. There went my chance for a future of
continued invisibility. I was stuck up front and center and

forced into chit-chat with whatever dreg passed my desk, and all seemed to be dregs who passed my desk.

The sales reps were no more, no less than their title suggested. Basically, full of shit and lots to spread around–especially if you worked for Bernice. They all needed to get on her good side and they figured I was their way in.

"Well, look at you, blonde bombshell. Aren't you God's gift to the gray skies outside?"

Believe me, I was as gray as the day.

"Don't I get a hug from my favorite blonde buttercup?"

My hair was a dirty shade, just shy of brown, that enhanced itself into blonde from the mouths of these letches.

"You trying to keep us guessing with those long skirts, blondie? I know something's sizzling under all that linen."

The only thing hot under all that linen were heinous pantyhose. Dress code demanded the evil leg coatings. I was always pulling at my crotch to keep them up when no one was around or attempting to hide the runs that slid up and down my legs like skid marks.

And then, Bernice would saunter off the elevator in all her flaming glory with heels that raised her up to pint-size status, the stench of Georgio cologne permeating her like another outfit and the jangling of chains, bracelets and earrings announcing her arrival.

I shuffled papers around and look down while she passed. Within a few minutes I was summoned into her office. She'd already called in, by phone, her posse of shiny groupies, a select mix of media buyers that Bernice had chosen, who filed into her office each morning and seated themselves around her, giggling at the expense of some poor slob's soul, including mine, laughing whenever I came in. One hideous day they decided to turn their attention on me.

They loved to invite me in as an onlooker, but now I became the brief center of attention. Bernice looked around the room at the girls and raised one of her painted eyebrows. "Michelle's been getting the eye from Lester Shapiro. Maybe she'll stop wearing those feedsacks and get some action going from one of the sales reps. They'll do anything for a buck."

All the girls smiled, nodded their heads and made their routine comments.

"Could do worse, honey."

"Better than those white-bread yuppies with their five-year-old-mommy-parted-it-on-the-side haircuts. Get yourself a jew, honey, and you'll never be bored."

Bernice took over again. "Okay, Michelle. So, what does that make you? Well girls, I think we've got ourselves our very own honorary member. You know what that means? That means keep your mouth shut and your eyes open and report everything back to us." The girls laughed and nodded again. Bernice continued. "And wear some goddamn jewelry. You're embarrassing me. Stop slouching and put on some heels! You like Lester? I can get you a date with any of these deadbeats, just say the word and it's a done deal."

This was worse than Bernice's loathing. I was now a pet. Their token goy.

It happened just like that. I was one of the pack. I was the weak one that remained relatively invisible. I now sat in on their morning meetings when they scoured over their parade of bad dates, new jewelry, hair stylists and good manicures. They snorted cocaine right off the rating books, which were the so-called "bibles" for a media buyer and held all the latest rating numbers for each television show. Bernice said doing lines of coke on the books was the only way to raise the ratings. At least the books got some use. I hadn't seen her open a rating book, and I was sure that was what buyers were supposed to do. Whether in Bernice's coven or not, buyers were expected to produce. A few of them did what Bernice did. They gave all their work to their assistants. Those select assistants would come bitching to me about what a waste case their buyers were and why couldn't they get a raise or a promotion, but I wasn't adverse to the extra work. It was the only way to move up the money ladder. I worked some nights until midnight and the weekends when Bernice was under the gun from her superiors. But when I got out, I really got out. Bernice came through with the goods. I got tickets to every show that came through Chicago. Prince, The Cure, Peter Gabriel, The Talking Heads and even Aretha Franklin, who played at a small theatre, totally high on something and forgetting the lyrics, but I didn't care. I was out there and it was great. Bernice bought me, just like all her jewelry and short-term boyfriends. This was way better than working the 7A-3P shift at the Holiday Inn in the Holidome in Skokie, Illinois. I was downtown Chicago now, and I planned to stay.

*   *   *   *

When something alters slowly, it isn't seen right away. There is a movement within the structure that slowly diminishes its fortification. An outside force must be the catalyst for this inner transformation. Molecules start to battle and separate from each other and the process of disintegration has already begun long before we become aware of it.

I didn't notice any changes at first. Bernice made her own personal appointments and so, for a time, I knew nothing of doctors or tests. I continued to work long hours and continued to harass Bernice to teach me how to buy television and radio commercial time, until one day she just up and complied. This should have been my first clue. She didn't want to lose me now that I was trained to take care of all of her crap. Our work partnership had become symbiotic. I knew what she needed before she even asked. We had created a smooth, unspoken connection. Now, she was suddenly willing to teach me to become a media buyer. I just assumed that she figured sooner or later some other buyer was going to teach me and I'd be moving up with or without her help, which had been my long-term plan anyhow.

This was the late eighties, before everything became computerized. Buyers were still doing everything by hand. I sat across from Bernice in her office while she prepared the playing board. And that's what it looked like when she was finished. She sat taping pages of long graph paper together into one huge mosaic of empty sheets that spilled out over the desk. It was a long and delicate process, as she had to keep her sculpted nails from tearing the pages and the tape from damaging her top-coat of the manicure.

Once the cutting and taping process was over, I was asked to remove the latest Arbitron rating books from the shelf. A few were already on her desk and I knew what they'd been used for. Bernice bought television commercial time for the biggest markets in the country, because she was the head of the department.

We started with Chicago, of course. She got her array of markers in various colors and fanned them out between her fingers. She wrote out the client at the top of the graph map in black marker. This one was for Burger King. She then had me name off each television station as she lined them up down the page, each with their own special color. She had me sound off each sales rep that represented each station in the market. She had a comment for every one of them as she wrote their names.

"David Rhenquist: NBC."

"He'd slaughter his mother if he thought he could squeeze a little more cash out of me. White trash strutting around in Calvin Klein suits. Of course, he's got NBC. I'll have to throw him a bone, at least. Who's next?"

"Adrian Flataux: CBS."

"Cheap prick. He asked me out once and took me to the fucking Olive Garden. He does have beautiful eyes though. Have you seen them? Greener than cash. A girl would die for those eyes. He'll fight to the end, but you know who wins in this office? Next."

"Miriam Schwartz: ABC."

"Did you see that new fur she was lathered in? Big fucking deal! I have more expensive underwear than that patchy meat pelt. Next!"

"Neil Sharp: WFLD."

"Not a bad one. The guy's thankful for anything I drop his way and he always sends a humungous bouquet of flowers afterward. I love that! We'll make sure to overrate him just to fuck with Rhenquist. Next."

"Antoinette Valenti: WGN."

"All bones and long as hell, but what a face. I think she's six feet tall, at least. She was a runway model for Ford before she became a rep. I like her. She's a bulimic, you know. Heads straight to the john after every lunch we've had and lets it all rip. She's a cigarette-coffee girl mostly. You can tell by the yellow teeth. She's a beauty and smart as hell. Great stories from the modeling days. We'll give her more than her share as well. Okay, next step: give me the shows, ratings from the book, and the rep's name again."

"Cosby: Number 1 show: 17 rating. That would be Rhenquist."

"I'll give the bastard a 6 on that one." Each rating point was worth thousands and thousands of dollars. If the Arbitron rating book showed that Cosby had received a 17 rating, then the buyer usually gave a 17 rating as well. These numbers had been calculated by thousands of households across the country and tabulated to come up with each particular rating number. A buyer might negotiate with the rep down to a 16, maybe a 15, but never lower than a few points. I looked up at her in horror, but she was busy with her markers and could care less.

I knew from the other buyers that all their charts were supposed to be written up with a #2 pencil, so that when the buyer negotiated with the rep, the number could be changed easily with an eraser. Bernice didn't care. She made her own rules. She rarely changed her initial choice of random numbers for the ratings. She based it all on her likes and dislikes of the reps, and they tried to battle with her, but like I said, she always triumphed. She held the Burger King money in her well-groomed hands, and there wasn't much they could do. A few of the braver reps had made complaints against Bernice, but they never won. Why? Because she saved the clients, like Burger King, a hell of a lot of cash by maintaining her witchdom.

That was what it was all about. The bottom line was always what it was all about, and the higher-ups loved Bernice because she spent less money than any of the other buyers, by far, which meant more cash in H.R. Bingaman's and the client's pockets and the client's continued dedication to the agency. Agencies were always maneuvering to get top clients away from their competitors, but Bernice was a unique weapon that H.R. Bingaman utilized and no other top agency had privy to.

Bernice and I continued on with our system. I read off the programs, the Arbitron ratings and then repeated the rep's name. No matter what the Arbitron rating was, Bernice had her own special number. Some numbers were actually higher than the rating book's, but those were specifically for the independent markets that were much cheaper anyway and the reps that she preferred. Why? Because they adored her when she gave them extra points and the network reps, who expected the high numbers, had to grovel for their points. Bernice enjoyed giving to the underdog, if for nothing else than to enrage the alpha dogs.

And once her radiant chart had been mapped out with a rainbow of colors, it was time to make the appointments with the sales reps to come in and negotiate with Bernice. I was in charge of making the calls and setting up the meetings with each rep without getting in the way of Bernice's hair appointments, manicures and luncheons. She had different reps take her out to lunch everyday. The favorites, of course, were given the nod, when I asked her. But when I came in her office and told her someone like Rhenquist was on the line and wanted to take her to lunch anytime, anywhere, she flipped me the international sign of rejection. It was my job to tell the guy to fuck off in an inconspicuous manner, so that he still had hope, when in fact he didn't have a chance in hell.

*   *   *   *

The tell-tale signs were slowly lining up in front of me, but I was only twenty-two years old at the time and didn't consider disease or illness an option, unless I was calling in sick due to a hangover. Bernice was thirty by then, which seemed old to me, but not old enough to get seriously sick. That was left for nursing homes, grandparents and soap operas. Seven of us ate lunch in the conference room and watched "All My Children" religiously. There was always some cute, young thing dying of a slow, lingering disease that never killed her good looks or mussed her make-up, but gave her husband good reason to commiserate with the hot nurse that he ended up smacking lips with in the hospital broom closet. Then beeps and blips from the machines around the dying wife's bed would suddenly change their tune into that steady flatline and nurses and doctors would come flying into her room just as the wife was about to die off, still pancake tan as ever, leaving the husband with overwrought guilt, one tear running down his cheek and an audience who now despised him.

I walked into Bernice's office one day and found her with her pocket mirror open, caking on another layer of mascara. It was the red rims that surrounded her eyes that made me wonder if she'd been crying. She barked at me to close the damn door and get out, which I did, but I was haunted by a look I had never seen on her before: fear. I was quite familiar with it from my own reflection in the mirror. I had studied its many facets.

* * * *

As things evolved and I became a permanent member of Bernice's morning posse, I started to notice changes. Bernice would say her usual biting, yet funny remarks about someone who could never defend himself. He was never in the room, but instead of the usual group consensus, one or two of the girl's started to undermine Bernice's comments.

"Well, I don't think he's so bad. We had lunch the other day and he even gave me a sample of some good coke to take to the bathroom. He's getting to be one of my favorite reps in the line-up."

"Yeah. I thought about setting him up with my cousin, Rachel. He's not bad looking and he's certainly not cheap. He's always bringing me little presents. I might have gone for him if I didn't have this fabulous ring already." She waved her finger out for everyone to see, as if they hadn't seen it a hundred times already.

"Are we talking about the same guy?" asked Bernice. "Rhenquist? With the rat tail snaking out the front of his pants? Please girls, compose yourselves. I can't believe what

I'm hearing. Have you lost all sense of decorum?" Bernice snorted.

"Really Bernice, you're way too hard on these guys."

This kind of chit-chat had never happened before in my presence. I could see looks exchanged behind Bernice's back. It felt as if a mutiny was in the works.

"How about you Michelle? You never open your trap. What do you think of Rhenquist?" asked another one.

Now the ball was whipped at me. Everyone turned my way, including Bernice. A smirk generated from Bernice's burgundy lips as she awaited my response. No one expected much from me, but a deflection from the intensity in her office. I smiled back at Bernice.

"How many of the mouths in this room have been sucking on that rat's tail? Let's see." I looked around the room with my finger to my lips.

Bernice threw her head back and roared with laughter. "Oh, this is priceless," she cried. "Have you girls been giving nasty Rhenquist an oral fixation through his Calvin Kleins?"

The girls rolled their eyes and looked at their watches and got up to leave. This time, Bernice won. There would be other times when it would not be so easy. But Bernice always had the final word.

"Now get out of my office and go generate some cash. We don't have time for this bullshit." She flicked her wrist, took off her earring and picked up the phone.

* * * *

Rumors propelled their way around the office.

"Did you notice Bernice is actually looking green? You can even see it through all those layers of base and powder she wears. I really feel for her."

"She looks like my college roommate did every Sunday night, gorging on pizza and then purging it up in a bathroom stall."

"Did you see her hair today? It's like a fucking Doris Day wig in brunette. Who does she think she's kidding? Everyone knows she's sick."

I had pretty much figured it out, but didn't let on with anyone else. I made excuses for Bernice. She wasn't sick. She had meetings to attend and appointments outside the office. The truth was that Bernice had always prided herself on attendance. Anyone who called in sick was weak or hung-over. She didn't tolerate it in anyone else and since I had started working for her I rarely called in. I was too afraid to face her battery of insults over the phone.

"Oh, little Michie's sick? What? You went out to your Panda Lounge too late last night and downed too many shots? God, you goyim can drink! Don't give me that sick crap. Just jump into one of your potato sacks and get your ass in here. We have a lot of work to do." And then she'd hang up. The scary part was that she was usually right. I was too hung-over to face reps and phone calls and all those

128

Arbitron ratings jumping off the page at me. I just wanted to lay on the couch, eat popcorn and watch soap operas.

The day I heard about the wig, Bernice finally called me into her office. She was standing with her back to me. A few of the girls were around her. The morning meetings had dropped off months ago for no reason that I was let in on, but then the posse never told me much anyway. This particular day one of the girls actually had her arm around Bernice. I'd never seen that before. Bernice was obviously not your touchy, feely sort. She even did those fake-kiss-in-the-air things with some of the reps at the parties. I'd never seen anyone touch her. When I came in the office one of the girls closed the door behind me. I stared at the back of Bernice's head. I could see why someone had made the Doris Day reference. Bernice's real hair was no flip job. It was a close-cropped haircut that she'd had since I'd first laid eyes on her. The girls were trying to convince her of the wig's natural beauty.

"It looks great on you."

"They did a great job styling it to your face."

"Really natural."

Bernice lifted her arms to stop them. "Okay, okay. Let's see what Michelle has to say. I can read her like a book." Bernice turned and faced me. She was translucent beneath those layers of make-up. There was nothing hidden now. My puny, little battles were exposed in her trembling lips. The fear in her glistening eyes propelled me forward into that long stretch of deceit and compromise that kept the endless daytime dramas going and me as far from the core of myself as I could get. She was the damn mirror of my own reflection–raw vulnerability. She smiled and threw her arms up in the air and sang, "Ta da." I stared at her. I think I smiled back, but it was too late. Tears coursed down her face and she told everyone to get out, but me. We both sat together in silence and cried.

In a soap opera, time moves from crisis to crisis. There is no down time. No sitting on toilets, staring at walls, getting stuck in traffic or riding elevators up and down, back and forth, to and from a job that you hate. Bernice's illness propelled forward like a soap opera.

You have breast cancer.

You go through chemotherapy.

Chemotherapy makes you wretch.

You lose weight and feel nausea all the time.

Chemotherapy does not save you.

Your hair falls out successfully.

You wear a wig or a scarf on your head.

You have an operation.

You lose a breast.

An ugly scar sits where the breast once was.

You now wear a lopsided bra with a pad stuffed into the empty side.

The operation does not save you.

You are going to die at the age of thirty.

The sickest part of it all was that while Bernice's body was rebelling against her, so was corporate America. Whatever power she once held was draining through her fingers like sand. Her superiors who once praised her for saving them all that cash were not interested in her demise so much as theirs. One by one they came down to her office, whenever she could make it in, to see how she and her work were faring. I was sweating it out at my desk, day and night, to keep Bernice's workload on track but it wasn't enough for them. I got to hear it all after they left.

"So Bernice, how are you feeling?" Bernice would bellow in a deep bass, mimicking the vice-president's voice. "Did you get that American Airlines package finished? We really need to get that one back to them. Oh, by the way, I've given the New York market to Alicia Bennett. I think you have too much on your plate at this point. Now you take care of yourself and let me know if I can do anything for you?"

"So Bernice, how are you feeling? Listen, we've gone ahead and given the Chicago market to Rebecca Silverstein. It'll give you more time to recuperate."

And it went on and on until she was just buying one or two small markets to make her feel like she was still doing something. The posse made only obligatory visits to Bernice's office at this point. I could see the guilt on their faces. They felt bad that she was sick, but they were still vying for her markets.

So, in the end, it came down to Bernice and me. The token shiksa goy had become Bernice's confidante, and the person I'd been scared to death of was now scared of death. There was no reason to lie anymore. We both knew that.

"It's all going to be such an overwrought production. I'm glad I won't have to participate. At least I'll be laid out in all my glory in a mahogany box, adding to the garishness of it all," laughed Bernice. "No more hammering away at these damn reps. I did give them a hell of a beating though, didn't I?" Bernice had stopped hiding her tears from me and they would slide down freely on our last days together. "Can you see it? All those fake waterworks marring all that expensive mascara? It'll be more dramatic than the Academy Awards." Bernice took a tissue and wiped her eyes. "There'll be Rhenquist, that ground swill, wearing his finest Calvin Klein's. You know that subtle pinstripe suit he wears to all the parties? That's the one. His hands will be folded and his head down like he's praying for me when he's really praying Silverstein will give up more of the cash than I ever did. He's already working her. I see bouquets of flowers on her desk every week. It's really barf material. I didn't need any chemo to feel the nausea rising in my throat whenever I walked by her office." Bernice had a faraway look in her eyes. "No. It'll be pure torture for them to get through the service, but you've got to be there." She looked at me and smiled. "At least somebody will enjoy the show. Wait till the Vice-Presidents get up there one by one to give their little speeches." Bernice moved back to that baritone voice.

"Bernice Mendelsohn will be sorely missed. She was a huge asset to H. R. Bingaman and there is no one who could possibly ever replace her." Bernice rolled her eyes. "Yeah, the bastards have already replaced me and I'm not even in the ground yet."

I didn't know how to react while Bernice gave me a blow by blow of her funeral to come. I could see it all like a film. There was no bullshit when I was with her. She had now become the only person I wanted to be with.

*   *   *   *

Then, like a soap opera, I was sitting at her funeral. The funeral home even looked like the cheap backgrounds for a soap opera–the coffin at the front, the over-zealous crying and wood paneling everywhere.

I found a seat at the back of the room. It was crowded with all the familiar advertising faces, and up front were the real tears of her family. I'd never met them and I regretted that. People were still filing in and as they moved past me I saw it all as if Bernice was sitting next to me replaying it. There was Rhenquist wearing the pinstripe suit. He was walking arm and arm with Silverstein whispering something to her. They found their seats and then I watched in awe as he clasped his hands together on the seat in front of him and leaned forward with his head down. I didn't know whether to laugh or cry. When the ceremony began I didn't listen to the Rabbi give his sermon. I watched the parade of caricatures in Bernice's play act themselves out. There were the Vice-Presidents lined up behind the family who, at some point, went up one by one to share their monotone grief. It was like watching "All My Children," but this one was a rerun. I could feel Bernice soaking up all the drama she had prophesized. Tears rolled down my cheeks. Bernice had probably seen these coming as well.

*   *   *   *

We had the day off that afternoon. I walked home and sat on the couch staring at the walls. Then I saw it. It was smiling at me from the table. I grabbed Mr. H.R. Bingaman's pumpkin head, ran for the window, opened it up and let him fly. I watched him fall three stories down until he smashed into a million orange shards on to the cement below. I closed the window and sat back on the couch. I took a cigarette out of the box on the table and lit it. I kicked off my shoes and then ripped the pantyhose right off my legs and tore them to shreds. That felt good. I got up again and went to the bedroom. My top drawer was full of them and I pulled them all out. With the cigarette hanging out of my mouth I took the stash to the bathtub and piled them all up. I lit a pair at the bottom and soon the whole taupe colored mass was blazing like a bonfire. I watched the toxic pile leap higher in flames with the acrid smell of plastic burning.

About the Author

Meg Tuite's writing has appeared or is forthcoming in over 50 magazines, journals and presses including 34th Parallel, One, the Journal, Hawaii Review, the Berkeley Fiction Review and Boston Literary Magazine. She is the fiction editor of The Santa Fe Literary Review and Connotation Press: An Online Artifact. She has a monthly column "Exquisite Quartet" at Used Furniture Review. She lives in Santa Fe, NM with her husband and a menagerie of pets.

Check out her blog at http://megtuite.wordpress.com.

Made in the USA
Charleston, SC
18 June 2011